An Account of the Implausible Life of
Ryden Brown

By E Provost

New Alexandria
CREATIVE GROUP

For Mom,
who thinks this is better than it is.

And for Shadowcat,
who can't read but I love her anyway.

First Print Edition

Produced by New Alexandria Creative Group

Sonoma County, California

©Copyright 2020 E Provost

www.NewAlexandriaCG.com

Available via Print on Demand wherever books are sold.

ISBN: 978-1-64715-000-6

Also available as an Ebook through most outlets.

ISBN: 978-1-64715-001-3

Cover: Ryden's Journal by Elisabeth Provost

Table of Contents

1

Grandpa Ryden's Untimely Demise

Lucas Brown never really understood the phrase "untimely demise." It implied the existence of a *timely* demise, scheduled for a date convenient to you and your loved ones. A demise all planned out ahead of time, the mourning done in advance, and once it ended, it would be back to business as usual, everything moving along according to a predetermined schedule.

There was no such thing as a timely demise. Death was always untimely, and could only ever be untimely, so the modifier was entirely unnecessary in Lucas's opinion.

Although, perhaps Grandpa Ryden's demise wasn't all that untimely, as demises go. The man was about a hundred years old, and he'd lived a good, long life, full of love and prosperity. But it was untimely to Lucas.

Growing up, he'd always thought that his Grandfather would outlive them all, despite being the oldest member of the family. He always seemed younger than he was, more sprightly than he should be, and far more up-to-date than a hundred-year-old historian had any business being. He was like a member of a younger generation, trapped in a boomer's body, an oddball, to be sure, but that was part of the reason everyone loved him.

Everyone *used* to love him.

Then came the untimely demise.

And now he was gone.

Lucas thought that two days after his death was too soon to be rummaging around his attic, but his mother and older brother insisted that he should see if there was anything that should be brought to the funeral.

"Like letters," his mother had said. "At mom's funeral, we read all the letters she wrote to people. Dad read some of the love letters they exchanged; it was so sweet. Look for something like that."

Of course Lucas had to be the one to look. He was the one living in Grandpa's house. He was the one who'd volunteered to take care of Grandpa in his old age, not that he needed much taking care of. They mostly just goofed off, binged shows on Netflix, played board games, even went laser-tagging once, but Grandpa made Lucas promise not to tell his mother.

He felt like he should have known something bad would happen. Should have predicted that Grandpa would fall to his death trying to take down Christmas lights by himself while Lucas was out getting groceries. Except he couldn't have known. Grandpa wasn't sick, or frail. It was an accident. A fluke. It could have happened to anyone.

Sometimes people just fall.

Sometimes people just die.

Usually in an untimely fashion.

So Lucas was brushing away cobwebs and trying not to kick up too much dust as he searched box after box in Grandpa Ryden's attic. Behind the boxes of Christmas ornaments which he had stowed away last month, he found a box which contained every single picture Grandpa had of his wife, Eileen, faded photos that had once hung in his home, their frames gathering dust, albums of wedding photos and event photos, even SIM cards from cameras, all packed away in a neat box of Grandma Eileen.

Lucas had wondered why there were no photos of her. They must have been too painful for her husband to look at after she died, but he couldn't help but wonder why they were still in a box in the attic after all this time.

A large trunk under the window was full of costume pieces from practically every era. Lucas remembered seeing Grandpa wear some of them, sometimes at the historical reenactments and renaissance fairs he loved like a prisoner nostalgic for a freer time, but sometimes just around the house. Once, Lucas saw Grandpa dressed from the 1940s, staring out the window, like the protagonist of a romance novel, longing for a loved one just out of reach.

Another box was full of newspaper clippings from the last eighty years, and printouts of articles. If there was a commonality between them, Lucas didn't see it, probably just articles that struck Grandpa as interesting.

In a smaller box, he found the love letters his mother had mentioned, which Grandpa Ryden had read at his wife's funeral. Lucas grabbed the box of letters and was about to climb down the ladder and out of the musty attic when a book caught his eye. The book was an old, leather-bound journal, with the name Ryden Brown imprinted on the cover, along with the image of an hourglass.

Lucas opened the cover and flipped to the first entry. It was dated April 05, 2192.

Lucas didn't read further for a moment, contemplating how the first entry in this clearly aged journal could have been written over a century in the future. Perhaps it was a science fiction story Grandpa Ryden had written in his younger years. Lucas found that unlikely, however, as his grandfather was a devout historian and openly abhorred science fiction as a genre, saying it was all "more fantastic than any myth or legend." Lucas pushed the thoughts aside and read on.

April 05, 2192

I have found myself waking up in a different place than I fell asleep for the past four mornings now. That in itself would be strange, but the curiosity is all the more incredible for the fact that I have also been waking up in a different *time*.

The first time, three days ago, it was in a women's boarding house in 1953. I was awoken quite abruptly and unpleasantly by a screeching woman, then chased out by several more women wielding weapons which varied from broom to high-heeled-shoe. I never realized how sharp a stiletto was until one hit me square between my shoulder blades.

It was a newspaper which clued me in to the change in era. First of all that a newspaper was even being sold, because I had never seen a real print newspaper before in my life; even as a history major, I'd never had need of one. The scans in the library databases were always sufficient for research purposes.

The boy on the corner was selling newspapers for five cents. I would have bought one, but I didn't have any money in my pajamas, not to mention that nickels haven't been manufactured in almost eighty years. I suppose that even if I had had money on my person, it would have been dated from modern day, and therefore not valid as currency so far in the past.

Thankfully the news boy was forthcoming with the date, even without me buying a paper; it was November 07, 1953. I spent the largest part of the day freaking out.

The second day I woke up in a motel room, in bed next to a woman who was very much naked, though thankfully, I was fully clothed. I had even thought to fall asleep in day clothes stolen from a department store, in case the unfortunate time-jumping situation repeated itself, so I wouldn't be caught in an unfamiliar time in my pajamas again.

The alarm clock on the nightstand displayed the date: December 26, 1997. I think it would be safe to assume that the woman in the bed had taken a liking to someone at a Christmas party the previous night. Or . . . the previous night for her anyway. I'm just glad I managed to sneak away from the motel without waking her.

I did not enjoy my time in 1997. The only public computers were at an Internet café, and they ran slower than a dying turtle, and I couldn't get any useful information from them anyway as the internet was in its infancy, so it had only a tiny fraction of the knowledge it has now. Also, I had trouble figuring out how to use such an outdated machine. It wasn't worth the hassle.

As much as I'm loath to admit it, I couldn't find answers at the library either. All the books about time travel were pure fiction in the nineties, making it a fool's errand. After my experience I can confidently say that 1997 was a complete waste of time.

The third morning, I woke up in a cell at a monastery. I still cannot be sure of the exact date of the third morning, but I can be quite certain that it was earlier than 1536, as that was the year when monasteries were dissolved. I believe the year was 1508 or close to it, as that was the latest year I saw in any of their records, and based on the weather I estimate that it was early spring.

The monks did not try to force me out as the women at the boarding house had in 1953, nor was I afraid of them, as I had been of the woman in my bed in 1997 and what she would do to me if she woke up and realized that I was not the person she had fallen into bed with the night before.

They did ask me where I had come from, and why, and I did not have an answer for them. The truth would have been too fantastic, but I couldn't very well lie to a group of monks. So I told them I had come from far away, sent by a force beyond my control. They believed that meant I had been sent by God, some thought I might even be an angel in disguise.

They asked if there was anything I needed, fed me some of the blandest food I'd ever tasted, and some of the bitterest wine. I asked if they could supply me with a journal before nightfall, and they agreed immediately, despite the fact that parchment was rare, expensive, and difficult to make at the time. I suppose there are perks to people thinking you're a divine being. The sun had just dipped below the horizon when one of the monks presented me with this very journal.

I don't remember when I told them my name, but I must have at some point, because it's pressed into the cover. It's even spelled correctly and everything, as opposed to some silly, old-timey spelling like *Riydaen Braunn* or something equally Chaucer-esque with too many letters. I also don't know why they decided to put an hourglass on the cover, although I suppose it *is* appropriate.

I wonder if they knew . . . perhaps God spoke to them or something. The night I spent at that monastery was surprisingly comfortable, all things considered, though, once again, I found nothing to explain my peculiar plight of sleep-time-traveling.

That brings me to the present, or rather, about three years into the future, after the turn of the decade into the 2190s. I called my family, who said they had not seen me in all those three years and believed me to be dead. I did some research on an *actual* computer, rather than a junky 1990s one, and found a few possible, if unlikely, explanations for my time-travel problem, but no solutions.

It may be a result of a natural extratemporal-field which has bonded itself to me for some reason. Or it could be due to one of those studies I signed up to be a subject for at my university last semester for extra credit and spare cash. It might be aliens. Probably not, but you never know. It's important to examine all possibilities.

It's also entirely possible that this is something completely different. That I will never find out what's causing this, and I'll never be able to stop it. Who knows when I'll pop back up in a time where my family is still alive? I may never see them again. And even if I do, three days for me was three, long years for them.

I shall keep searching, and I shall record my findings and my experiences in this journal, which I have managed to keep with me by tucking it underneath my shirt while I slept.

With determination,

Ryden Brown

The journal intrigued Lucas greatly. It didn't seem like the type of fiction Grandpa Ryden would write, and Lucas didn't think he would ever name a character after himself, either. If it wasn't so incredibly unlikely, Lucas might've even thought that everything written in the journal was true, and that his grandfather really was a confused time-traveler chronicling his experiences.

If nothing else, reading the journal was a good distraction, a good way to pass the time, so Lucas tucked it under his arm, along with the box of letters, and carried them both down the ladder out of the attic. Then he made himself a cup of tea and settled himself on his favorite armchair to read the rest of his grandfather's journal, which was already proving itself to be as queer as the man who wrote it.

2

Enter the Stranger

Situated comfortably in the huge armchair in the living room, which Grandpa Ryden had bought specifically for him when they'd stopped by a garage sale walking home one day and he'd found it to be the most comfortable chair his rear-end had ever had the pleasure of resting on, Lucas opened up the old man's journal once again.

The second entry was dated in the past, 1941, just as the first bout of soldiers would have been shipped out to join the fighting overseas. There were a couple of newspaper clippings tucked between the pages of the second entry. One was an article about a big New Year's Eve celebration in Times Square, the other was a *Popeye the Sailor* comic strip.

December 31, 1941

I woke up on a park bench in New York City this morning when a police officer bopped me with his baton and told me to move along, because I couldn't sleep there. I got up and walked away, and thankfully he didn't try to follow me. That was the first time I didn't wake up in a proper bed so far.

Once again I found the date on a newspaper, this time as I passed by a newsstand on Broadway. I was able to buy one with some spare change I found in the 1950s that was thankfully dated before 1941.

I also had a lovely conversation with the vendor, whose name was John Davis. John had three children, a girl and two boys, and he told me, "I know fathers are always supposed like their sons best, because boys are more fun than girls or some such nonsense, but I think my boys are too rowdy, and their mother lets them get away with too much when I'm not around.

"Suzie, on the other hand—that's my daughter, Suzie—she and I read together in the evenings after I get home and before she has to go to bed. She's only seven years old, but she's smart as a whip, and I don't have to pretend to like her cooking like I have to do with my wife's sometimes. I like her better than my boys. I'll admit it. She's nicer, and she's not half as obnoxious."

I told him that I thought girls were just as good as boys, and that there was no shame in acknowledging when your children need discipline and when they deserve praise, regardless of what gender they may be, then I made the mistake of adding the phrase: "boys, girls, or anything else."

He laughingly asked me, "What else is there?" and I didn't know how to respond to that. I forgot how close-minded people were about that sort of thing in this time period, where liking his daughter more than his sons was something John thought of as terribly strange.

I settled on saying, "You never know," then nodded a hurried goodbye and strode off to read my paper somewhere else before he could question me further.

The newspaper, which was called *The New York Times* (just like the 'news' website from my home-time, which runs mostly exaggerated political exposés, pseudo-scientific predictions of the future, and overenthusiastic, heavily biased sports reviews), was running lots of stories about the war in Europe, which America was just beginning to get involved with. It also had a story about a huge New Year's Eve celebration being thrown in Times Square to "bring in the new year and send out the soldiers with a great big hullabaloo." That's a good word: hullabaloo, and I'd never seen it before I read that article.

I've decided a few things, now that I've realized that I'll probably just have to get used to this whole uncontrollable-time-bouncing thing. Firstly, I've decided to refer to the 2180s, the time I came from and the time in which I did most of my growing up, as my "home-time," the same way I would refer to San Diego as my "home-town."

Secondly, I've decided that I'm going to perform some experiments to figure out just how this time-bouncing actually works, starting with "do I have to be asleep for it to happen?" New Year's Eve seems as good a day as any to test the answer to this question.

Thirdly, I've decided that I like newspapers. They feel nice in my hands, because the paper is thinner and more flexible than the pages of a book, and it makes a pleasant wrinkling, ruffling sound when you move or fold it. Newspapers are also full of interesting reports about all sorts of things like finances, and sports, and businesses, and who was born, who got married, and who died. Things that I never even thought to wonder about before, like what a man named Arthur Daley was randomly thinking at the year's end. And there are a whole two pages dedicated to entertaining little illustration strips like fun-sized comic books with no discernible plot, that are just there to make you laugh.

I am going to the Times Square hullabaloo tonight to celebrate with the rest of New York, even though in my home-time it's actually October 10th, mostly because I want to experience a hullabaloo, which I don't think I ever have before, or if I have, I didn't know at the time that it was a hullabaloo.

Based on the context of the article, I assume that a "hullabaloo" is something like a wild party, or perhaps a chorus of loud screaming involving everyone present, which sounds equally fun, but a great deal more cathartic than a party, if I'm telling the truth, especially given what I've had to deal with the past few days. It's like the worst jet-lag ever.

With interest,

Ryden Brown

January 1, 1942

I suppose I could start this entry with a joke about how I once again found myself in a different year this morning than I was in yesterday night, but I have other things on my mind. There are a few things I want to write about, but the first will be my findings in regards to the question: "do I have to be asleep for the time-bouncing to happen?"

The answer is, apparently, "yes." Time has progressed normally from one day to the next. It turned from a Wednesday to a Thursday, without any nonsense of finding myself in a completely different era after the change occurred. This discovery is about the least interesting thing to happen to me in the last 24 hours, however, because one New Year's Eve tradition is the same in the 1940s as it is in the 2180s.

I shall describe what happened in greater detail, mostly to reassure myself that it actually happened, because it was certainly the last thing I would ever have expected to happen to me in 1941 . . . or would it be 1942? (The turn of the new year has always been confusing, and the fact that I've woken up in a new year several times as of late is no help to me whatsoever.)

The crowd in Times Square consisted of quite possibly *thousands* of people. I generally consider myself pretty extroverted, and I like talking to new people, but the sheer quantity of partiers intimidated me still. I kept to the edges of the crowd—the hullabaloo, which I now know is, in fact, a wild party.

I popped in and out of stores and restaurants that were open very late for the celebration. I had myself a glass of champagne, which was weaker than I was used to, but more flavorful, and listened to live music played by a brightly dressed marching band which stood, un-marching, on a corner with the streets as tightly packed as they were. The band was good. They played swing music with a nice, loud drum-line and a ragtime rhythm that vibrated right through my whole body.

A man in a military uniform—many of the men wore military uniforms—whose name, I learned, was Frank, saw me tapping my feet and wiggling my shoulders to the music, and asked me if I didn't know how to dance, which of course I didn't. I didn't even know how to dance in my home-time, so of course I didn't know how to *swing* dance.

He called his girlfriend, Etta, over to help him show me, and the two of them taught me the Charleston, which is where you kick your feet out around to the side and then when you pull them back in you tweak your ankles (the ankle-tweaking bit is the trickiest). And they taught me the Balboa too, where you just kinda push and pull your partner around and around, back and forth, turning in a circle. And since those took me so long to learn, Etta told me I didn't really need to know much else, even if the Charleston was kind of outdated.

I danced a little while with them, and then with another girl, a redhead named Mary-Ann, who showed me how to do the Basket whip as well, which is where you sort of turn your partner around while pushing them away, and then whip them back towards you and back into the dance. Swing dancing really is just swinging everything around, your arms, your legs, your partner. It's much more aptly named than I ever realized.

When the band took a break, and I thanked Mary-Ann for the dance, she asked if I wanted to go get some booze, and looked confused when I declined.

"But I thought we were having a good time," she said. "Don't you want to spend the rest of the night with a sweet old gal like me?"

"No thank you, but I did have a good time," was apparently the wrong answer, because she glowered at me, snapped something that sounded like it was meant to be very rude, but since I don't know what a "nelly" is, or why she thought I was one, I can't say I was particularly offended by it. Etta noticed, and asked me if I was alright, and I said I was.

"If I'd'a been called a nelly, I couldn't'a been as calm as you," Frank said, angry on my behalf. "The nerve of that broad! Why if she weren't a girl, I'd boff her." He didn't tell me what "nelly" meant, nor why I should be offended by it. I'll have to look it up next time I'm in a year with internet.

"There's no reason for that," I told him. He looked like he was about to grumble something more, but he didn't get the chance because we were interrupted when a perfect stranger shouted my name.

"Ryden!" he called. "I've been looking all over for you!" He couldn't have been talking to anyone but me. I know, because the name Ryden did not exist in the 1940s, and also because a moment later, he pulled me into a hug, and upon releasing me, told Frank and Etta that he was sorry, but he had to steal me away from them. Then he grabbed my wrist and dragged me off.

I was too surprised to protest, or try to break away. The man obviously knew me, even though I was sure I had never met him before in my life. He kept dragging me along, until he finally stopped in possibly the only empty spot in the vicinity, an alley behind an Italian restaurant, though not for long as he shortly took me up the fire escape onto the roof of the two story building. There were lamps along the street, which illuminated enough for me to get a pretty good look at the stranger.

He was pale, not just white-passing like me, but like, *white*. He must have been Irish or something. He was also nearly two feet shorter than me, shorter than any of the men I'd met in the 40s, actually, and his hair was light brown, and not slicked back like most of the other men, but loose around his face. Even though everything about him had an odd sort of quality which I'm not entirely sure how to describe except that he seemed like if pastel were a person, his eyes were blacker than newly pitched asphalt after rain. Like many others, the strange man wore a military uniform.

"I almost didn't find you in time," he said, and smiled at me, then reached toward me gently, and took my hands into his. I looked back and forth between the stranger's face and our joined hands, utterly confused and at a loss for words. A thousand voices started counting down from ten.

"Nine! Eight! Seven! Six! Five! Four! Three! Two!"

"It's midnight," the stranger said, taking a step closer. Then he dropped my hands, stood on his toes, swung his arms up around my neck and pulled me down into a kiss.

The distant crowd screamed, "One!" and, "Happy New Year!" and started singing "Auld Lang Syne" but it was so, so far away to me.

He kissed me!

He was a good kisser, too, *oh my God!* I would normally be pissed about someone doing something like that without my consent, and definitely still don't approve, but oh my God! I'm sure glad we were all alone on that rooftop, because the way he kissed me, we might both have been lynched. He grinned as he pulled away, looking for all the world like it was the best thing that he had ever done, then honest to goodness, he *skipped* away. While I stood there in a state of shock, he slid down the fire escape and left me there.

That was a New Year's Eve kiss I won't forget anytime soon.

With astonishment,

Ryden Brown

3

Cross-Temporal Déjà-Vu

After he finished reading the third entry, Lucas could only stare at the wall, shell-shocked for a moment. Was Grandpa Ryden gay? But he married a woman. They had a daughter. Could he be bisexual, or something like that? It seemed like it came from out of the blue at first, but after he'd had a moment to consider, he realized it really shouldn't have been as surprising as it was.

He'd sort of thought that nothing about Grandpa Ryden *could* surprise him anymore after he'd built a one inch scale, fully functioning Roman battlefield replica spanning his entire backyard, complete with flammable ammunition for the catapults, and stone walls made of actual stone, then said it looked just like he remembered it. Lucas was eleven at the time, and his older brother Gregory was fourteen, and the three of them had waged a war on that battlefield that nearly burned down the shed.

Their mom had banned anything with fire after that, but Grandpa had no shortage of mischievous miniatures and other educational shenanigans. The viking longswords had been particularly fun, and the World War One trenches they'd all dug in Grandpa's backyard, until they hit a sewer line. That stunk.

Then he was certain he couldn't be surprised by anything else when, after he'd just moved into Grandpa Ryden's house to become his caretaker, he discovered the old man rode a real, live horse to and from his workplace at the high school. Apparently he didn't have a driver's license, and the 4H/FFA/agricultural enthusiast students loved Bike—that was the horse's name, and it was short for Bichael, because Grandpa Ryden was a smart-aleck.

Lucas had definitely not expected to see the animal when Grandpa told him he rode his bike to work every day. Bike was still alive, as far as Lucas knew, but he had no idea what had happened to the horse. Perhaps he'd gone to a ranch, or maybe he was staying full-time at the school. Despite being ancient, Grandpa Ryden had never actually retired, but he had had Lucas drive him the past year or so because his butt couldn't take horseback riding anymore.

When Grandpa Ryden had dressed as Angelica Schuyler from *Hamilton* for Halloween two years before, pink dress, curly wig, bustle, and all, then, *then* Lucas was *sure* nothing the old man could do would surprise him anymore. And yet, there he sat, reading a diary that, for all he knew, he reminded himself, could be complete fiction, and even dead, Grandpa Ryden had a few more surprises left for him.

Once Lucas had recovered his wits, he turned the page. He couldn't quite explain why, but he felt suddenly like he hadn't known his grandfather nearly as well as he'd thought. Even if this was fiction, and he was beginning to have his doubts that it was, however mild those doubts were, it painted his grandfather from an angle Lucas had never seen before.

The Ryden in the journal was young and confused, and still figuring things out. He wasn't the same man that had built battlefield replicas with his grandsons, and taught history to teenagers, and played the *Hamilton* soundtrack exclusively for a month as soon as it was released. None of that had happened yet. The Ryden in the journal was a broke college student just trying to deal with the crazy curveball that life had thrown him, and he had no idea what was going on. All he knew was that he wasn't going to let it get him down.

March 16, 1774

It's just my luck that I'd manage to miss my birthday by one day in all this time traveling nonsense. One detestable day! Granted, it's 1774 and I haven't actually been born yet, also my birthday in my home time was just eight months ago, so I haven't actually aged a year, but still. It's enough of a justification that I missed the chance to make all my usual Ides of March jokes, birthday or no birthday.

I woke up in a hammock on a boat bound for America. Evidently the hammock belonged to a member of the crew, and when he found me, he dragged me to the captain, who threatened to throw me overboard, believing that I was a stowaway—which I suppose I am, in a manner of speaking.

Eventually the captain decided to throw me in the brig, rather than the sea. I'm not sure if that was the preferable option, in all honesty. We're in the middle of the Atlantic Ocean, and I hardly have the strength or stamina to swim for longer than an hour or so, let alone the weeks it would take to get to land, so I guess I should be grateful for my life, but this brig is absolutely abhorrent.

Everything is damp, for one thing. The iron bars of my cell are quite rusty, and it reeks like must and mold. There's a crack in the wall, near the ceiling, and every so often as the boat sways on the sea, salt water splashes through it. I know it's somewhat absurd to think a crack so small is any danger to the ship, but I do worry about sinking. I've never been on a boat before. Also there are rats.

I always thought I didn't mind rats at all. My older sister has kept pet rats for as long as I can remember, and they never bothered me any, so I guess I thought that applied to rats in general, but it doesn't. The rats in this brig are nothing like Avalia's pet rats. These ones are dirty and have matted fur and crooked whiskers, and they're aggressive, and they hissed and spat and snarled at me when I didn't even do anything.

A boy came down after the first hour with some fresh water. He didn't tell me his name the first time I asked, saying that the captain had warned him not to talk to me much in case I tried to trick him into releasing me. Evidently the captain thought there was a high probability that if I did try something like that, it would work. I assured the boy that I had no intention of leaving my cell, abysmal as it was, and even if I did manage to escape, I had no place to go. We were in the middle of the North Atlantic.

The boy nervously told me his name was Peter. He seemed to be afraid of me, and I asked him why.

"Pray pardon, but you are exceptionally large, taller than anyone else onboard, and you look much stronger than most of us be, as well," he told me. "It's just that . . . you do intimidate me."

In my home-time, I'm exactly average height, and I've never been tall enough to be found intimidating for it. However, it is a proven fact that people have gotten larger over time. I never thought about that until I started waking up in the distant past. At just over six foot four, I'm taller than anyone I've met in the past, so far.

That's not entirely true; in 1997 I did meet one person as tall as me, the librarian, but he told me he'd never met anyone as tall as him before. But I was more than a foot taller than any of the monks in 1508, taller than anyone I met in 1953, taller than any of the soldiers in the 1940s, much taller than the man who—I already mentioned that, I think. I don't need to repeat myself.

Anyway, I'm not used to being so tall that people are intimidated just by my appearance. Actually I don't think anyone's ever been intimidated by me. I'm not exactly an intimidating person. I'm bookish, and I don't work out, and I'm too nice to scare anyone, and too friendly to hurt anyone. If I look strong at all, it's more genetics than anything. Now that I think about it, I really should exercise more, but I digress.

I told Peter that I wasn't nearly as intimidating as I looked, and that actually I was a bit of a nerd. He didn't know what nerd meant, and now I wonder when the word was invented. It's funny how little most people know about words used all the time. I told him it was a Spanish word that meant "weak or harmless person." He didn't look like he'd know enough about Spanish to refute me, and he didn't, but he didn't look like he totally believed me either.

I asked him if he knew the date, and he did, but he scrunched up his eyebrows when I asked the year. We talked for a bit. He told me about his home in England; and his plans in the new world; and his mother, whom he missed; and his younger brother, who died of smallpox just a few months before Peter set sail.

I must remember to get vaccinated against smallpox at the earliest opportunity. I hadn't thought about it, since in my home time the disease was eradicated two hundred years ago, but it's very important to be vaccinated, especially since I don't want to contract a disease in the future and expose people in the past to something they can't cure or vice versa. I wouldn't want to be responsible for an epidemic.

Peter left a little while ago when the captain barked something at him that I didn't quite understand. Another thing I never really considered about the past is how differently people talk. I never thought about how much accents change over time, and how much language really evolves. It's terribly fascinating, but I do wish I didn't have to experience it first hand. I wish I could just study it at home.

I shouldn't think about home. It won't do me any good, and I must make the most of this thoroughly incredible thing that is happening to me. I've come up with a few more questions to test, so I can gain a better understanding of this time-bouncing thing.

I've already confirmed that I have to be asleep to move in time, so my next question is: will I move in time every time I fall asleep? I will test it by taking a nap around midday, and seeing if I've time traveled when I wake up. My theory is that I will, but if I don't, it might mean I have to enter REM sleep, and a short nap won't do that.

I'd also like to know when the earliest and latest times I can travel to are. So far the earliest time has been about 1508 and the latest was 2192. I will make sure to keep track of every date I land in, even though I might never know the exact limits of my travels.

Another question I have is: do I always have to wake up on a surface that people use for sleeping? So far I've only woken up in beds, except for the hammock today, and the park bench in 1941, and I know people sleep on park benches sometimes, if they don't have anyplace else. Could I possibly wake up in the middle of a lake? Or in the sky? Or underground, even?

Also: Is there a reason for the places I wake up? I've woken up mostly in America, but I was definitely not in America when I woke up in the monastery, and I'm not in America now.

And this last one isn't really relevant to the time-bouncing thing, but I'd like to know who that man was . . . the one who kissed me. I could have sworn I saw him today, met his ink black eyes for a split-second when I got dragged to the captain, but he looked away, not acknowledging my presence. It couldn't possibly have been him, of course, he hasn't even been born yet. I must have imagined him, or simply experienced déjà-vu; that's the only explanation. I have been thinking about him a lot. He was . . . so strange, even for a stranger. I want to know more about him. I want to know how he knew me.

But for now, I must try to get some sleep in his dreadful brig.

With disgust,

Ryden Brown

4

The Truth About Miracles

June 7, 596

I saw him again, that bastard, and I know he saw me too because he gave me the stink-eye and turned on his heel. I know it wasn't him. It can't have been him. It is literally, one hundred percent, entirely impossible for it to have been him, but it *was*. I'm sure it was. Stupid Mr. Kissface is here in North Africa in 596, one thousand three hundred forty-five years before the first time I met him and he looks exactly the same. Maybe he's a time traveler too, but then is it a coincidence that we keep ending up in the same time and place?

Whatever. I don't want to think about him. He ticks me off so much I forgot that I'm trying to use formal voice in these journal entries. What a pain . . . oh well.

This is the earliest I have landed so far. I woke up on a reed mat on the floor of an empty home, and rather than stick around to meet the occupants, I snuck away, and eventually found myself heading to the most crowded place I could find, drawn to the hustle and bustle. It was a market of some kind, perhaps a bazaar.

No one in this time or place speaks English, and to be frank, I am not sure if it has been invented yet, and certainly modern English hasn't, so even if they did speak English, I wouldn't understand. It's a good century after the fall of Rome, but I managed to find a merchant who knew some Latin, like the monks at the monastery. I took four years of Latin all through high school, so there is one ancient language I can understand. I never imagined it would be all that much use to me, just thought it was interesting, but here I am.

The merchant was a wide man, but very short, as with everyone in the past, and I believe he said his name was Fahd, although, I'll be honest, I might be mistaken, and if I am not, I might be misspelling it. Either his Latin was heavily accented, or he spoke it properly, and I still had trouble understanding him, but since I have no way of knowing what a proper Latin accent sounds like, I may never know the answer.

He sold fine jewelry which I did ever so wish to buy—opportunities to possess genuine ancient accessories in pristine condition are, after all, exceedingly rare—but I, unfortunately, had no money, and I did not wish to steal from someone so helpful to me. Such is my constant plight of late.

When I inquired about the date, Fahd told me that it was "the seventh day before the Ides of June in the year that is four from the end of the century 500." That is, supposing that I am translating correctly, and that the merchant can be trusted to have kept good time, the seventh of June, in the year 596, or thereabouts.

As for where I am . . . I'll be honest, I don't know for sure. Fahd did say that this city was called Punt, but I've never heard of it before, and have no idea where it is. I deduced that the location is somewhere in the north of Africa, because Fahd mentioned that this city is a major trade partner of Egypt, but that doesn't necessarily mean I am correct in that assumption, only that I have a factual basis for it.

I cannot further my experiments without a decent watch, with which I can set a timer, so for now that's all I have to report. With luck, I'll wake up tomorrow in a time in which people can harness electricity.

With irritation,

Ryden Brown

February 29, 2100

I feel as though there must be some sort of irony to be found in someone that jumps through time miraculously landing on leap day, but I'm not in the mood for such humors.

I've stolen a wristwatch, capable of setting alarms, and timers, and functioning as a stopwatch, so I can use it to further my experiments. In my situation, such a device is a necessity, but I do wish I didn't have to steal it. Given my circumstances, not being in any time for longer than two days so far, it would be impossible for me to get a job and earn money to pay for things, so the only way to get what I need is by stealing. I am, in essence, a time traveling hobo, which does not present me with all that many career paths.

Despite the fact that it would be impossible to convict me for my crimes, I still feel bad for playing the "desperate times call for desperate measures" card, even if I don't really have a choice. I feel like a criminal, and worse, I actually am one.

Anyway, all this to distract myself from the more pressing sentiment, which is that I saw the man again. He didn't see me this time. At least, I don't believe he saw me. He did close his eyes and smile for no apparent reason when I caught sight of him, which was odd, or perhaps it wasn't. I don't really know anything about him, do I?

I don't believe it is possible for this to be coincidence anymore. If I see him again, and I feel quite confident that I will, I plan to confront him and demand to know who he is. I must confess I am immensely curious about him, and I'm working myself into a frenzy with wonder. I've nearly convinced myself that he may not be entirely human.

I did test my first question, set an alarm for an hour and took a nap in an Ikea store, which was rather revolting to be perfectly honest, but I sleep where I can without being arrested. I did not travel in time. This result was unsurprising as I anticipated that I might not. Next, I will take a four hour nap, which will be long enough for me to enter REM sleep, and see if that makes a difference. In the meantime I'll be looking for an empty motel room to sneak in the window of, or a for-sale home, or anyplace more pleasant to sleep in than an Ikea display bed.

I really am becoming quite the scoundrel, aren't I.

With shame,

Ryden Brown

September 2, 1826

The man's name is Nikolas Miracle.

I suppose I shouldn't jump the gun like that. I should give it some lead up, like when I wrote about the kiss. I spent the entire entry building up to it beforehand, but mostly I just want to express my ire at the fact that my mystery man is literally named Miracle. That said, I will back up now and explain how things went down in greater detail.

I woke up in a tenement with about five other people in the room, and it was disgusting. The president was John Quincy Adams, and the newsboy on the corner was forthcoming with the date and a few headlines which told me more or less that I was once again in New York, and that a ship called the USS Vincennes was going to depart tomorrow with the goal of being the first US warship to circumnavigate the globe. It seemed like a bit of a dull purpose to me, but I supposed life was boring in 1826, and they just didn't have anything better to do.

Finding myself once again lacking funds, I did not buy a paper, as much as I wanted to. I would have liked to pay the ha'penny the boy asked for, but I didn't have anything dated before 1900, much less a ha'penny, and the boy had a mean face, and looked like he would beat me soundly in a fight, despite our sizable height difference.

"Can't afford a paper, Ryden?" a voice asked from behind me, and I could hear the smile on it. "Don't worry, I'll buy it for you. I know how you enjoy newspapers." He handed the newsboy a ha'penny in exchange for the paper, which he then handed to me, saying, "You don't mind if I have it when you've done with it, do you? You can't take it with you, after all."

I was too surprised for a moment to do more than thank him, despite my plans to demand his identity, and when he walked away, he looked like he expected me to follow him anyway, so I did. Then he said, "It's lovely to see you again, my good man, care to join me for breakfast? My treat, of course."

"'Again'? So you do know me?" I said, which I know was stating the obvious, but I was still reeling a bit from him approaching me, rather than the other way around as I had planned. "Who are you?"

"Who am I? Oh, is this the first time we've met?" He asked,

as though it were a perfectly reasonable question, and he had no idea whether or not he'd met me before, despite somehow knowing my name and my fondness for newspapers, which I have yet to tell anyone about.

"Well . . . no, we've met before, but I didn't catch your name last time."

"Ah, of course, that must have been the . . . nineteen-forties, you told me?" He looked like he was going to say more, but his face suddenly got very red and he coughed. "My name is Nikolas Miracle—that's N-I-K-O-L-A-S, not 'C-H'. I like my 'K'—and Miracle is just spelled like the word."

"How do you know me?" I asked.

"Oh, we've met from time to time." He smiled at his own joke, blush fading. I'll admit here, privately, that I thought it was hilarious, but I didn't laugh at the time, because I was grumpy, and didn't want to give him the satisfaction. "So, breakfast? I have a friend around here that owns a diner, best eggs Benedict you'll ever have, and the pastries his wife makes are to die for, hypothetically speaking of course." I let him drag me by the arm to a little diner tucked into a corner a few blocks away.

He was rather . . . dorky. I expected him to be serious, or maybe the mysterious, quiet type, but he wasn't. He was sweet, and friendly, and he laughed at his own jokes, and sat a little too close to me, and rested his leg against mine under the table, and asked me about the newspaper articles and smiled a lot. Actually, he was adorable.

We spent the day together, wandering around New York, and he took me to see a play at the newly built Bowery Theatre, and let me choose which one. I selected *A Comedy of Errors*, mostly because the other one was a black-face minstrel show, which I had no desire to sit through. The show was nice, and fun, but nothing innovative. We sat near the back, and Nikolas laughed louder than anyone, and in some parts, he was the only one to laugh, as if at some private joke that no one else was getting.

He made me smile a lot, more than I have since this whole time-bouncing thing began. I wasn't worried all day, and I actually enjoyed myself, and it didn't even feel forced. I liked spending time with Nikolas. Now I only wish that I'd approached him sooner.

At the end of the day, he offered me his bed, saying he didn't mind sleeping on the sofa for one night, since he knew I'd be gone by morning. I didn't ask how he knew that. As I write this, I'm sitting on that bed, which is quite comfortable, and I don't particularly want to fall asleep. I don't want to go.

With uncertainty,

Ryden Brown

5

Beware the Toils of Love and War

Reading the journal put a lot of things in perspective for Lucas. It explained why Grandpa Ryden never seemed to consider the legality of things, for one. Lucas often thought it was as though his grandfather forgot that certain laws even existed, especially the ones regarding theft and piracy. It explained why Grandpa Ryden had a tendency to take short naps, and not sleep through the night, and where he had gotten the watch he always wore, which was clearly very old, but had features that Lucas was quite certain had not been invented yet.

As he read entry after entry from the old leather journal, Lucas became more and more convinced that it was real. There were things in the journal that Grandpa Ryden couldn't have known about when he wrote the entries, described with accuracy that couldn't have been achieved through guesswork, and the journal provided reasons for all of Grandpa's oddest behaviors.

Thinking back, Lucas remembered things he'd written off as Grandpa being old and weird that really weren't old fashioned behaviors. Things like always asking for someone's preferred name, and not calling anyone 'sir' or 'madam' or 'miss' or 'mister' unless they asked him too. Things like how, when Lucas visited as a teenager, he was never asked about a girlfriend, because Grandpa always asked about a 'special someone' or used other gender nonspecific terms. Things that even the most PC people don't always do.

Then there was the time he was sure he could remember Grandpa Ryden singing "thank u, next" by Ariana Grande while he was grading papers, a year before the song was released, then forgetting a line, getting frustrated, and trying to google the lyrics only to grumble about "what year was it released in, then? Stupid song." His proficiency with Google and other modern technologies was also unusual for a man of his age.

The more he thought about it, the more Lucas found himself accepting the journal as non-fiction. He had always thought of Grandpa Ryden as younger than any of them, ahead of his time, so it made a lot of sense if he was from the 2180s. If Grandpa Ryden truly was a man out of time then it was hardly a wonder everyone thought he was so timeless.

One thing really bothered Lucas, though, and that was the fact that he could swear he'd heard the name Nikolas Miracle before, but for the life of him, he couldn't remember where. He tried looking up the name online, but the only results were about a song called "Miracle" by a guy named Nikolas Metaxas, and an ancient religious order of Russia about a Saint Nikolas the Miracle-Maker, neither of which were things that Lucas had heard of before.

Perhaps it was his mind playing tricks on him, or perhaps it was an inkling of an old, old memory that he'd long since forgotten. He might've heard the name mentioned in passing, or maybe he was thinking of the miraculous story of Saint Nicholas that always got told to small children on Christmas. Perhaps it would come to him later. Perhaps it would bother him forever. Perhaps he should ask his mother about it. She would probably know. Ryden was her father after all, wasn't he?

The next few entries were much the same as the last one. Ryden would wake up in a strange time, find Nikolas Miracle, and spend the day with him. They played croquet in 1901, which Nikolas won, then went out drinking. In 2139, they spent the day in a nuclear fallout shelter, apparently due to a threat from North Korea which Ryden had known about, but Nikolas was nervous about. Oddly enough, Nikolas wasn't worried about himself, but rather expressed his desire to fight the enemy face to face, rather than hide from their bombs. In 1611, Nikolas took Ryden to see a production of *The Winter's Tale* in the original Globe Theatre, and evidently it was a live adolescent polar bear which pursued Antigonus off the stage in Act III.

He also tested his REM sleep theory, and discovered that it would appear he was correct in his hypothesis that he had to enter REM sleep to time travel, and also that it didn't have to be night for the time-traveling phenomenon to occur. Nikolas, Ryden recorded, was disappointed by his experiments, because it cut their time together short. Lucas was quite sure that Nikolas was in love with Grandpa Ryden, and that he had meticulously planned all of their activities as dates, but somehow Grandpa Ryden hadn't realized that yet, according to his journal entries, and it was rather frustrating, because it was obvious he liked Nikolas that way too.

The next entry had an old, yellowing envelope tucked between the pages. It was addressed *To: Ryden Brown, From: Nikolas Miracle*, in a handwriting which was not Grandpa Ryden's. The seal was partially broken, but not completely, and the top was partially ripped, but not enough to get the paper out. It looked like someone had started to open it several times, before deciding they weren't going to read the letter after all.

June 5, 1944

I woke up on a boat again—a warship this time—in a soldier's cot, and Nikolas was the one who woke me. He was standing over me, along with a handful of other men in World War 2 military fatigues, and Nikolas was smiling, but they all had an aura about them that said they were on edge, and I would soon learn why.

"Rise and shine, Ryden, m'dear," Nikolas said, and I pulled off the blanket and sat on the edge of the low bed. "Didn't expect to see you again so soon."

"Ya dear?" questioned a man with a midwestern accent; the name on his jacket was *Johansson.* "Who is this fella, Miracle? What's he doin' in Peters' cot?"

"Oh Ryden here's always waking up in strange places," Nikolas answered offhandedly, coal-black eyes twinkling with a private joke. "Where were you yesterday, darlin'?" When he called me darling, I couldn't help but glance nervously at the other soldiers. I didn't want them to get the wrong idea about us, especially given the environment.

"We went to see *The Winter's Tale at the Globe,*" I told him, which surely didn't help refute any ideas the other soldiers might have been getting.

"Ah, I remember that."

"And where am I now?"

"You're in Peters' cot," said another man whose jacket said *Jones.*

"That's not what he meant, Jones." Nikolas shook his head, almost chuckling. "You're on a US military vessel on the English Channel. It's June 5th, 1944, and General Eisenhower recently announced that Operation Neptune has been delayed until tomorrow due to bad weather conditions. You got good timing, one day later and you'd have been stuck with us, storming the beaches of Normandy."

"I might've liked to see such a historic event," I said, then it dawned on me that *seeing* it and *fighting* in it were two very different things, and Nikolas was quite right about my luck in this situation. "Actually, I'm not much of a fighter, so maybe it *is* for the better that the operation got postponed."

"A Goliath like you's not much of a fighter?" scoffed one of the men. He wasn't wearing his jacket, but I later learned his name was Harlan Bryant. "How tall are you, anyway?"

"Six-four." Several of them whistled in astonishment.

"Your poor mother," joked Harlan, and his buddies laughed, but I didn't find it all that funny. Always being considered some kind of giant has got to be one of the worst parts about all this.

"We were just dropping off some stuff before we headed to the mess hall, care to join?" Nikolas offered, and I accepted. Before I befriended Nikolas, I'd always had trouble getting sufficient meals, but since we became friends, he's been more than generous in making sure I get enough to eat. I feel bad that I can't do very much in return.

We spent the day not doing much of anything as all the preparations for Operation Neptune had been completed already, since it was supposed to take place today. Jones shared his comic books around (he had every edition of *Captain America*), and Harlan joked around with everyone. I flipped through some of my earlier journal entries, hard to believe it hasn't even been two weeks since all this began, and remembered the last time I was in the forties, dancing at the New Year's hullabaloo, and asked the guys what "nelly" meant. A few of them shot awkward glances at Nikolas, before Harlan finally told me, in his own words, that it was forties slang for a male homosexual. Made sense now why that girl Mary-Ann had called me one when I said I didn't want to go with her, and why Frank thought it was so rude.

I asked Nikolas in private why they had looked at *him* when I asked, and he told me most of them knew he was a nelly, but that none of them would do anything because they also knew that, despite his small stature, he could and would beat them up. He told me he had a few more lifetimes of experience under his belt than any of them, and I'm not entirely sure what he meant by that, but I suspect I'll find out soon enough.

At some point in the day, all the soldiers took the time to write letters to be given to their families if they died during the operation, which should have been very morose, but they all seemed to be in good spirits. When Nikolas wrote his, rather than giving it to their commanding officer, he sealed the envelope and handed it to me.

"I don't have any family left, and all my friends will live or die by my side on the battlefield tomorrow," Nikolas said. It was hardly a happy statement, but he was smiling softly. "You're the only person I'd want to give this to. Stick it in that journal of yours, and as long as you'll see me again, don't open it." I agreed.

I know that Nikolas does not die tomorrow, and I have no doubt that I'll see him again. I don't expect I'll be reading his letter for a very long time, if ever.

It's lights out soon, and they all have a big day tomorrow. Nikolas has offered to share his cot with me, and . . . while I'll privately admit it was a tempting offer, I refused. It won't be the first time I've had to sleep on the ground since this time-bouncing thing began, and I doubt it will be the last.

None of them did more than roll their eyes when Nikolas said I wouldn't be there in the morning. I suspect he may have told them stories about me as they haven't been particularly surprised by my presence since they first found me in Peters' cot this morning.

I've wished them all the best of luck tomorrow, and told them all they're sure to win, and to make sure they know what's happening in case something goes wrong. I do hope they all survive. I've only known any of them for a day, but they're good men, and it would be a tragedy if they died, even to save the world.

With Concern,

Ryden Brown

Lucas put the journal face down on the coffee table, taking the old, yellowed letter into his hand. He didn't know exactly how long it had been since Grandpa Ryden wrote that journal entry, but it must have been very, very long ago, and in all that time, the letter remained sealed. Grandpa

Ryden always held out hope of seeing Nikolas again. Taking a deep breath, Lucas thought to open it himself, but stilled his hands before they could tear open the envelope. The letter wasn't meant for him.

Curious as he was, he knew he shouldn't. Nikolas had written it just before he planned to go to battle, when he thought he might die, and it was sure to be very personal. Plus, Lucas suspected it might be a love letter, and one just didn't go around reading their grandfather's personal love letters, even if one *did* read their grandfather's personal journal. He sighed and picked the journal up from the coffee table. Tucking the letter back between the pages of the 1944 entry, he flipped the page and resumed his reading.

6

The Inherent Romanticism of the Sea

It was several entries later when Grandpa Ryden finally admitted to himself what Lucas had been suspecting since the entry from New Year's Day, 1942. Lucas had always thought of his grandfather as more observant than the journal would suggest, but he also knew that it was sometimes harder to see things in oneself than it was to see them in others.

April 22, 1688

For the third time, I woke up on a ship, a great old brigantine with tattered sails and splintering woodwork. I didn't think it was a warship, but it had clearly seen its share of battle. The ship, it seemed, was called *The Blackbird*, and the crew were not fond of strangers. They found me in a hammock and dragged me to the top deck, loudly vocalizing their plans to throw me overboard.

There were four of them on me, dragging me up, and I can only assume that they felt the need because of my stature, though they were all armed, and I still hadn't done much in the way of improving my fitness, so I probably couldn't have held off even one of them.

"Captain Ferro!" shouted one, and a man with a short, unkempt, red beard, a tricorn hat, and a dark red coat hopped down from where he'd been sitting on the rails of the boat, his boots landing on the deck with a heavy thud. "We found this stowaway in one of the hammocks."

"We haven't docked in nearly a fortnight," the captain remarked, puzzled. "How couldst we possibly have missed a stowaway so large?"

"A large stowaway, say you, captain?" asked a familiar, smiling voice, coming up from belowdecks. "Now why dost that sound ring twice?" All of my anxiety melted away when I heard that, and my heart sang.

"Nikolas!" I greeted cheerfully. "I'm so glad you're here."

"Likewise!" Nikolas said. "I haven't seen thee in decades. Bastian, Quentin, Hamish, Nero, I beseech thee step away from him, if thou wouldst be so kind."

"Thou knows this man?" asked the captain.

"His name is Ryden Brown, and I do know him well," Nikolas said. He walked over to me and tried to toss an arm over my shoulder, but upon finding himself too short to do so, settled for resting his arm around my waist instead. I rested my own hand on his head without realizing, and his hair was soft. "He is a witch who dost travel through time as easily as he would dream."

"A witch?" repeated the captain.

"My witch," Nikolas corrected, and I felt my cheeks heat up at his words. I had never been anyone's anything before, outside of my family, and it felt nice to be wanted, especially since I haven't been able to stay in one place for very long. "And I'll not allow any harm to come to him."

"He's yours, then," the captain looked suddenly on edge, and I can only assume that Nikolas was glaring something fierce. "He will be thy responsibility, and no harm will come to him, as long as he sails upon The Blackbird, so says I, Captain Ferro. You hear me? Ye scalawags!"

"Ay Captain!" chorused the rest of the crew.

"Come, Ryden, I'll teach thee how to tie the rigging."

Nikolas taught me knot tying for a couple of hours. We just sat on the top deck, listening to the seabirds and the ocean, and tying sheet-bends, and fisherman's knots, and figure-eight follow-throughs for a while, talking and laughing.

"Miracle! Take your witch up to unfurl the main sails!" the captain shouted at some point just before noon. "Quentin and Lizzie! Take the other sail! Nero! Flavio! Bastian! Secure them as they drop!"

"Ay Captain!" Nikolas shouted back, along with the others whom the captain had called on. Then he taught me to climb the rigging and untie the knots which held the sails in place. It was up on the top of the sails that I knew for sure that I was sailing on a pirate ship. At the top of the mast, tied down so it didn't wave, was a black flag. When I asked Nikolas about it, he told me that it was their Jolly Roger, black flag, white skull and crossbones with a blackbird on the forehead.

I had no idea that Nikolas was a pirate. He had never mentioned it before, although I suppose it makes sense to hide the fact that he committed high crimes on the high seas, but I'm no less disappointed that he withheld the information from me. I've always loved pirates. I know that they were not the nicest people, that's a given, but I was going to take a special course on the history of piracy next semester at university, and I've always loved old pirate stories. Tales of people like Blackbeard, Ann Bonny, and Cheng I Sao, and of course pirate fiction as well.

It wasn't until lunch when I finally met most of the crew. There were twelve in all, and they introduced themselves to me over a meal which consisted of heavily salted beef, boiled greens, two-week-old pears, and of course, rum. The captain was named Edgar Ferro, and he was from North England, and had once been part of the queen's navy before his ship was taken by the previous captain in a particularly stupid battle. Evidently *The Blackbird*'s crew lost eight members before they finally managed to sink the navy vessel, which didn't even have anything valuable onboard.

Then there was Bastian Sand from Lancashire, who was the navigator, and Beck McAllen from Ireland, who was a medic, who looked like they could've been twins, or at least brothers, but made it very clear that they were not in any way related. Hamish Adair was Scotch, and he had a peg-leg. Nero Viola and Flavio Scotti were both swordsmen from Italy, and their English left something to be desired, that is to say I could barely understand either of them, and I don't think I was the only one.

Lizzie the Whirlwind AKA Elizabeth Walsh was the only female member of the crew, and quite possibly the most vulgar of the bunch. Their cook, whose real name I never learned, was a shy man only about three inches shorter than myself, whom they all called the lady, and the only person who seemed especially friendly with him was the deaf marksman Isaiah, who was in charge of the canons, and who sat next to the lady, and who seemed very gentle.

Then there was the first mate David Burroughs, who had come aboard *The Blackbird* at the same time as the captain from the same naval ship, and who had been the captain's friend since they both joined the navy. Lastly there was Nikolas, the second mate. He had been the second mate as long as any of them could remember, since before Captain Ferro, and even before several of the other crew members. They all called Nikolas by his last name, Miracle, even though the rest of the crew went by their first names. Nikolas assured me that it was pretty common for him, but he didn't tell me why. I did, however, learn that Nikolas is actually Greek, which I never would have guessed since he's so pale.

Not present at lunch was their lookout, Michael "Mousy" Kitt, who was only fifteen, and had come onboard as a stowaway the previous year, and been kept on because of his skill with climbing and rigging, as well as his exceptional eyesight. Evidently he'd become sort of their mascot. Mousy always ate meals separately from the rest of the crew, up in the crow's nest or somewhere else.

After lunch we worked. I helped Nikolas sand the rails which had been splintered in a few places in a fight a few days ago, and he told me that they cleaned like this once a week, and as much as they all complained, the captain just said if this were the navy, they'd be cleaning like this every day, and that a respectable ship had to be kept spic and span. Once we'd finished sanding, we mopped the deck using seawater.

That evening, after all the chores were done, the lady cooked another hearty meal, and we all drank rum, and then just after sundown, lanterns were lit all around the deck, and Bastian, Hamish, Flavio, Mousy, Lizzie, and Nikolas put on a commedia dell'arte style performance wherein four suitors were all trying to win the affections of a beautiful maiden, who was played by Mousy in a frilly dress, all the while trying to avoid her terrifying and evil father, whom Nikolas played.

In the end, Lizzie won the affections of the maiden, and she picked Mousy up and swung him wildly around, while he giggled uncontrollably, and Beck started playing the fiddle, and David pulled out a penny-whistle and everyone started stomping their feet and singing a song they had clearly sung many times before about happy lovers and victory. Nikolas asked me to dance, and taught me how to do a high-stepping jig which quickly wore me out, but it was so fun that I kept dancing anyway. I couldn't stop smiling. I had *never* liked dancing before, in fact I despised it, but I love it now.

Slowly but surely, the crew began to wind down. Beck handed his fiddle to Flavio, who played a slower melody which I recognized as a somewhat famous piece from a classical composer who, now that I think about it, is probably alive now, effectively changing the instrument from a fiddle to a violin. The dancing slowed, now only a handful of pairs swayed on the floor. Lizzie and Mousy, the latter still wearing his frilly dress, twirled and giggled. Isaiah and the lady danced quietly as well, off to the side. The captain and the first mate had a sort of dancing/wrestling thing that they were doing, and then there was Nikolas and I.

When the music finally stopped, I slipped cross-legged to the deck with a heavy sigh. Nikolas plopped down onto my lap, and without a thought I slid my arms around him. His eyelids drooped, but his lips were curled into a lazy smile.

"Awww, are ye two not the sweetest pair?" Hamish teased, poking Nikolas with his peg leg.

"'Zounds Hamish, leave us alone," Nikolas mumbled, then he nuzzled his head into my chest and was out like a light.

"Does he yet sleep?" Lizzie walked over to us, panting from all the dancing she'd done, and Mousy trailed behind, finally wriggling out of his dress to reveal a simple pair of trousers underneath. "'Tis a Miracle miracle. He always makes a fuss before he falls to sleep, tossing and turning into the wee hours."

"I think 'tis time we all head down to sleep," the captain said, and went to his quarters. I picked up Nikolas, careful not to wake him, and David led me to Nikolas' cabin. Apparently Nikolas preferred to sleep in the hammocks with other people around, but they thought it was better for him to have his own cabin, not that he ever used it. David and Lizzie also had their own cabins, and the lady and Isaiah shared one, and the rest of the crew slept in the hammocks. There was one more cabin which David said I could use if I wanted. I put Nikolas in his bed, pulled his blankets over him, and then just stood there silently staring, while David lit a lantern behind me.

"Just kiss him," David said, and when I turned I saw him roll his eyes. "'Tis clear that thou'r sick with wanting. None of us became as we are for to better control our impulses. We art pirates, and pirates taketh what they want, and regret not, so wherefore dost thou hesitate? If thou wants a kiss, then steal one." Then David shook his head and left with a sigh.

David was right. I do want to kiss him. I want to kiss Nikolas a lot. I think . . . that I might be in love with him. But I can't. Kiss him, that is. I won't be held responsible for loving him, but I can't make a move without asking first, and he can't give consent if he's asleep, so to kiss him would be wrong, even if he did kiss me without asking in the forties.

I was going to leave, find the spare cabin, write my journal entry and go to sleep, but just as I opened the door to leave the cabin, Nikolas reached out in his sleep, and asked me to stay, and I couldn't say no. I'll be gone in the morning anyway.

With anxiety,

Ryden Brown

7

How I Love Thee, Serendipity

It was about time Grandpa Ryden admitted it, Lucas thought. He didn't know why or how he had gotten so invested in the love story between his grandfather, and a man who was decidedly not his grandmother, but he had. And though he could see from Grandpa Ryden's point of view why he was hesitating, he also didn't understand it at all. All signs pointed to Nikolas feeling the same, and in fact, Lucas wouldn't be surprised if the man thought they were together already.

Nikolas was a peculiar fellow. He seemed to have a long, rich history—as a soldier, a pirate, a fan of theatre, and a kind fellow whose associates were all, inexplicably, a little bit afraid of him nonetheless. There was, without a doubt, a story there which Lucas sincerely hoped he'd discover through his grandfather's journal. He adjusted his position in the armchair, leaning back a bit more, and reached for his tea only to find the cup empty.

He got up and took a moment to make another cup, before resettling himself in the armchair, and reopening the journal. The next two entries were dated November 4, 1851 and July 10, 2076 respectively, and there was no change in his grandfather's routine.

In 1851, Ryden found Nikolas, who excitedly showed him his copy of the first ever *New York Times* newspaper from September, which Ryden had told him about before it existed; and in 2076 Nikolas took him to a new exhibit on greek theatre. Evidently they'd recently discovered a number of previously lost plays and reproductions of the scripts and costumes, as well as diagrams of what the theater and sets may have looked like, were on display in the Museum of Natural History in New York for just a month before they were to be moved to the Smithsonian.

Nikolas told Ryden about how much he'd been wishing he could take him to the exhibit, and when he did, Nikolas read scenes from the plays in the original Greek with all the enthusiasm he could muster, and though no one could understand him, they applauded anyway. He read a few in English, as well, translating as he went. The museum employees, Grandpa Ryden wrote, seemed particularly impressed.

May 31, 1983

I woke up in a bedroom which looked like it belonged to maybe a seven year-old-girl, and I am so very lucky that there was no such girl present, and furthermore that the apartment was otherwise empty because that would have been exceedingly difficult to explain. I've managed to come this far without being arrested, and I'd like to keep it that way. I was careful to make sure that no one was outside the apartment door when I snuck out.

I wasn't in New York, for some reason, and I worried that I might not see Nikolas because of that, but as it turned out those worries were unfounded, because I saw him at a grocery store where I planned to shoplift fruit or something for a late breakfast.

"Stop thief!" a voice shouted, the moment I picked up an orange. I jumped and whipped my head around with a start, only to see Nikolas there, laughing. "Alright there, Ryden? Didn't mean to scare you."

"Yes you did," I argued.

"Yes, well, it was funny." He shrugged. "I can buy that for you, I know you never have any money."

"Thank you . . . I feel bad that you're always buying me food. I wish I could do something for you, too."

"You do plenty," Nikolas waved me off with a grin. "I'm lucky if I get to see you twice in a decade, let me spoil you."

"But I see you every day . . ."

"You sure are lucky then, because I'm an exceptionally good-looking sight, and a joy to be around to boot."

"You're not wrong," I said, and I hadn't meant to say it aloud, but banter like that comes so easily with Nikolas that I spoke without thinking, which would have been more embarrassing if Nikolas hadn't seemed so happy about it.

"I was just thinking the same about you recently, ya big friendly giant." He didn't seem to be thinking much before he spoke either. "Say, do you know the *Star Wars* movies?" I did of course, my sister is a huge fan, and made me watch all thirty-something of them, including the side stories and the live action series. She tried to make me watch the animated stuff too, but I could only take so much, especially after the quality began to drastically decline. Still, the early ones were pretty good.

"Yeah, I watched them with my sister back in my home-time." There was no need to go into detail, especially since he seemed so excited about it.

"So you know them better than I do for sure, huh?" he guessed. He may have been wrong, actually, seeing as I only watched a handful of them more than once and wasn't nearly as invested as Avalia. "Well the third one just came out a few days ago, *Return of the Jedi*, and I haven't gone to see it yet. I saw the last one on opening day, but I've been hesitant—worrying about what happens to Han. Would you like to come see it with me? You've gotta promise not to give me any spoilers, though."

"I think I can handle that."

"Then help me finish grocery shopping and we can go this afternoon."

It was peaceful, grocery shopping with Nikolas. We talked about the time, and how terribly out of date my clothes were, and how it was a shame he couldn't get *The New York Times* since he'd moved out to California, but *The L.A. Times* was alright too. It had been a while since I'd done something so normal. That said, the only things I really know about the eighties came from horror movies set in the decade, so there were a few moments where I almost expected something gross and/or terrifying to appear out of nowhere, but nothing ever did. Or at least, nothing has so far.

The most surprising thing that happened was when we got back to Nikolas' house, arms loaded with groceries, and I thought I heard him say he wanted to kiss me. Sure that I had misheard him, I asked him to repeat himself.

"I said, I'd like to kiss you. But last time I tried you freaked out and got all uncomfortable and embarrassed, which was kinda funny, but also kind of insulting."

"What brought this on all of the sudden?" I asked him.

"Nothing sudden about it really. Like I said I don't see you that often, last time was almost twenty years ago, so of course I'd want to kiss you."

"What do you mean 'of course' you'd want to? You never said anything about—or . . . for me it's only . . ."

"Is something wrong Ry?" I have no idea when he started to call me Ry, but it didn't make me any *less* flustered, that much I can say with certainty.

"I've only recently been thinking that I might really like you . . . I'm sorry, I suppose in 1983, that's probably a strange thing to admit."

"'Only recently'? Haven't we been together since 1440-something when you couldn't understand a word of English so we spoke in Latin, and you fell off that horse?"

"I have no memory of that." I could feel my face heating up drastically, and I just knew it had to be bright red, but Nikolas mercifully didn't bring it up.

"How long have you been at this time traveling thing?"

"A couple weeks," I answered.

"Really?" His eyebrows shot up for a moment, then he chuckled and rubbed the back of his neck. "I forget sometimes that you experience things in a different order than I do. You said you liked me though, right? I'm glad that at least is still the case. I guess 1964 must have been earlier for you."

"I haven't been to 1964."

"You haven't? So then it happens after this?" His eyebrows pulled together in confusion, and he looked away in thought for a moment before he asked, "Then why would you freak out when I kissed you?" I had to think for a moment about what possible reason I could have for turning down a kiss from Nikolas, but when I remembered our first kiss in the forties, I answered his question with one of my own.

"Did you ask first?" He pursed his lips, thinking for a moment.

". . . No? I'm not sure."

"You've gotta ask first, Nikolas. Consent is important, even just for things like kissing."

"I see, so if I ask first, then . . . can I kiss you?"

"Y-yes." I'd like to say my voice didn't squeak, but I swore I'd keep this journal as accurate as possible, so I'll admit, with great embarrassment, that my voice squeaked quite horrendously. A moment later, we were at eye-level, and he leaned forward gently.

He did kiss me then, and to say it was as wonderful as the first time would be an understatement. This time, I knew who he was, and more than that, this time I was in love, and entirely willing. When he kissed me it felt like I really wasn't alone; like for the first time since all this began, I had someone who wasn't going to be gone the next day, who would stay with me. I was so happy I thought I might cry.

It was a long moment before he pulled away, grinning as before, like kissing me was the greatest thing he'd ever done, and I mirrored his smile as best I could, though I wasn't sure my lips could stretch that far. I wrapped my arms around him in a tight hug, and it was then that I noticed where he was standing. My mind must've been preoccupied when he'd climbed atop the coffee table in order to be tall enough to reach my lips, but I couldn't halt my laughter when I realized that even doing so he was shorter than me.

He griped at me for laughing at his height problems, but I could tell he wasn't serious. After that, he took me shopping for more fashionable clothes. Though I happen to like the nifty grey suit, blue button up, and saddle shoes that I got from the fifties, Nikolas said I looked like a stiff. I had to ask what that meant, and he said it was the same as a dead body, or a square. I also had to ask what square meant in the context, as well as zoilist, stupe, dorbel, stick-in-the-mud, and aniaros (pretty sure the last was Greek). After some frustration, he finally managed to convey that a stiff was a boring, uptight person.

Once he'd gotten me into some blue jeans, a leather jacket, a red t-shirt, and a pair of sneakers, he deemed me worthy of going out in public. First lunch, then *Star Wars: Return of the Jedi*, which was a great deal more fun to watch with Nikolas next to me, cheerful, and excited for his first viewing, than it ever was to watch with Avalia, cackling maniacally because she knew everything that was going to happen, and stroking one of her pet rats.

I never thought about it before, because that's just how my sister was, but I'm starting to realize that she really was rather strange . . . *is* rather strange, or maybe will be rather strange, once she's born. I must not think of my family in the past tense. I'll see them again, I'm sure of it.

I haven't anything else to report today. To be honest, I'm still reeling a bit from this morning. When all this first started, I don't want to admit it, but I was dreadfully afraid. I didn't know what was happening, and I didn't know anyone, and I didn't fit in anywhere. It's not easy to be a man out of time. I'm so thankful for Nikolas. Since we met, I haven't been as scared. I don't understand much more; I'm still confused by a lot, but I have someone who can guide me through it now. And for that someone to love me as much as I love him . . . well, at risk of sounding cheesy, it feels like a real miracle.

With contentment,

Ryden Brown

8

Between a Blessing and a Curse

The entries got shorter after that, some containing only the date and location he'd woken up, and Grandpa Ryden's handwriting had been getting steadily smaller as the entries progressed, eventually getting small enough that Lucas had to search for his grandfather's reading glasses. Apparently he'd realized that he had a limited number of pages, and eventually he must've run out, because there were several sheets of loose leaf paper tucked between the final page and the back cover.

In the next few entries he mentioned that he'd started to revise his sleep schedule so he could spend more than a day at a time in each era. Sleeping only short periods for two to three days, before going back to REM sleep for a minimum of five days. It was as safe and healthy as he could manage, given the circumstances, and more to extend Nikolas' time with him than anything else.

The next entry of note was dated just two days in the future, the day the funeral was slated to take place, and that knowledge filled Lucas with unease. As soon as he read the date, saw the length of the entry, he decided it was time to break for lunch, but grilled cheese and tomato slices couldn't delay the inevitable much. Stomach now full of dairy as well as dread, Lucas picked the journal up again, and started to read.

January 29, 2020

I woke up in a big, cushy bed, in a luxury hotel in my home town of San Diego, which was odd because usually I wake up in the same city as Nikolas, but I knew since he'd left New York he'd only lived in Los Angeles about two hours away. I suppose I must've been a bit bleary since it was my first REM sleep in two days, but as soon as I realized I was in San Diego, my first thought was that I had to get to LA to see Nikolas, rather than assuming Nikolas was there for some reason.

I found enough accumulated cash in my pockets dated before 2020 to buy a bus ticket to LA, and after acquiring a plum from a street vendor on the way to the bus station, I did just that. The ride was long and boring, but when I got off the bus, I didn't have much trouble finding Nikolas' house. I'd been there before, and LA isn't a particularly difficult place to navigate, even if one's watch doesn't have a GPS feature.

When I got there, I dug the spare key he gave me out of my pocket, and let myself in, only to find the place was empty—except for his pet tortoise Tetsudo (named for a Roman battle formation where soldiers mimicked the shell of a turtle by putting their shields together). Not knowing what else to do, I sat in the company of Tetsudo, read a book from Nikolas' shelf, and waited for him to come home.

It was nearly seven PM when he arrived, and the moment he saw me, he burst into tears. I don't believe I've ever seen Nikolas cry before, so needless to say I was worried. Before I could stand, he strode over to the couch and sunk onto my lap, bawling into my chest. I held him, and asked him what was wrong, but it was a long time before he could answer, I don't know how long exactly, but after a while he sniffed, adjusted himself so he was more comfortable, and told me, in the smallest voice I'd ever heard from him, what was wrong.

"I've just got back from your funeral, Ry," he whimpered, hands gripping my shirt tighter, as though he thought saying that might make me disappear, or drop dead on the spot. Everyone knows they're going to die, so of course I knew I was going to die *eventually*, but hearing Nikolas say it was jarring. To think that I'd be comforting my love after my *own* funeral was unreal, and I had no idea how to respond to the information. I couldn't think of a single thing to say, until Nikolas asked, "I'll see you again, won't I?" and I knew I had to reassure him.

"Of course you will, we meet several times in the next couple centuries at least," I said. "You haven't met my parents or my sister yet, and I have to introduce you, so we'll have to meet again. You may have to wait a while, but you'll definitely see me again. You can wait, can't you?"

"Yes my dear, if there's one thing I can do, I can wait." He said. His grip tightened even more, and I could feel his shuddering breaths. "I'm sorry for crying on you."

"Don't be. Crying is healthy, and there's no reason to apologize for it." Nikolas burrowed his face into my chest and I felt his tears soak through my shirt. Eventually he stopped shaking, and, rather than think about the fact that my funeral was today, I decided to ask a question that had been on my mind for quite some time, thinking perhaps it could take his mind off things.

"May I ask, Nikolas," I said, rubbing soothing circles on his back, "why do I see you in every time I end up? You don't have to answer . . . you might not even know—you know what, forget it."

"No it's alright. You see, I'm immortal," he told me, pulling his head back to dry his eyes on his sleeve. "Like you, I'm a man out of time. I was born in Sparta before the common era. I think it was three hundred . . . ninety something or eighty something BC by modern count? I calculated it once, but I don't really remember. I was a member of the Spartan army. You said you were a history major, so I'm sure you know something about that."

"Yes, I do . . . so . . . you're old, huh?" was all I could think to say. I had suspected that he wasn't a normal person, and immortal had been one of my theories, but I'd written it off as highly unlikely.

"Yes, I'm old." Nikolas chuckled softly and his lips drew up in a small smile. It was nice to see him smiling again. Despite what I had said, it hurt my heart to see him cry.

"That doesn't explain why I always see you though," I said. "I mean I could pop up anywhere, so why do I always pop up practically on your doorstep? And how'd you get to be immortal anyway? Does it have anything to do with why I time travel?"

"Woah, there, slow down, one question at a time." Nikolas sniffed against his residual runny nose and pursed his lips in thought for a moment before he spoke again. "Let's see, time is kind of tricky. It's not like one continuous event, but more like a series of events, and all those events line up end to end to make what we perceive as the timeline. It's not like a piece of string that you can loop around and cross over itself, that's why time travel is normally impossible. It's more like . . . like a bunch of magnets, all stuck together in a long line.

"You can force the magnets apart, but they always stick back together again. However, if you take one of the magnets, and turn it around so it's facing a different direction than the others, the magnetic poles repel each other. That's kinda what it's like when someone gets stuck outside of time. If another magnet gets turned around, then the two backwards magnets attract each other, and like with the rest of the magnets, you can pry them apart, but they'll just stick together again.

"That's us. When I became Immortal, the magnet that is me got turned backwards. I interact with time, but don't connect to the timeline, so I don't age. When you started time traveling, the magnet that is you got turned backwards, but because my magnet was also backwards, your magnet latched onto it. When you fall asleep, or enter REM sleep, or whatever, the magnets get pulled apart, but they get drawn together again at a different point in time.

"That's what I think anyway." Nikolas shrugged and closed his eyes, adjusting his head on my chest. He must've been tired from all the crying. "I took a class on time and relativity, because I was curious too. It was boring. The magnet thing was the only theory I could come up with that made any sense."

"So basically what you're saying is that objects out of time are attracted to each other?"

"Mhm. Romantically, in our case." Nikolas smirked, not opening his eyes. "But yeah, that's pretty much it. I can even kind of sense your presence when you show up. I wake up some mornings and somehow I just know that I'll see you. Usually it's on my worst days, when I need you the most, or when something exciting happens that I really want to share with you. I think that strong emotions like that might have an affect too, like they supercharge the magnets or something so you get drawn to specific days. Might be reading too much into that one though."

"I see." It did make a sort of sense, but there was a reason I decided to major in history and not time theory or some other scientific field. I never was scientifically minded enough to figure out things like that on my own, but the way Nikolas explained it I thought I understood. "So, how do the magnets get turned around?"

"Divine intervention? Cosmic coincidence? Dumb luck? Beats me." Nikolas yawned and opened his eyes to look at me. "How'd you start time traveling?"

"I still haven't figured that out yet." He snorted. "Well how'd you become immortal, then?"

"Oh, that? Well, I'm old and wizened now," he said in an exaggerated old man voice, "but I was young and stupid once. I mean I'm a Spartan, there's a reason we're known for our army and not our education system." I quirked an eyebrow at him and prompted him to explain further, dropping the impression. "Well, the long and short of it is: I thought I was hot stuff, and I did something crazy that no one else was willing to do, somehow managed to save a bunch of people, and the gods offered me a reward, anything I wanted."

"The gods?" I couldn't stop the sarcasm from seeping into my voice. "The Greek gods don't exist."

"Well not anymore," he scoffed right back at me. "It's kinda like time travel doesn't exist yet." I rolled my eyes, but let him continue. "Anyway, I was fresh from a major victory, and brimming with hubris, so I asked the gods for eternal youth. But see, I'm not a demigod or anything, I was just some random dude who happened to be in the right place at the right time, with enough skill and reckless courage to pull off something no one in their right minds would even think to try, so they couldn't just hand over immortality.

"I don't remember the details of why they had to jump through so many hoops to grant my stupid request, but in the end it was Apollo who proposed the solution. Rather than granting me immortality, Apollo allowed me to live independently from the sun. The sun moving in the sky is what makes time pass, so if I was immune to the sun, I would also be immune to the passage of time, and therefore I wouldn't age, which sounded good to me."

"Sounds like the logic of someone who believes their gods live on a perfectly climbable mountain and never bothered to check."

"Yeah, laugh it up McFly, where were you yesterday? 16th century England? Ancient Rome?"

"Is that why you're so pale, even though you're Greek? I always wondered about that. I thought you might be Irish when I first met you."

"Well that's just insulting," Nikolas scoffed. "But yeah, that's why. Nobody really considered the other consequences of basically being *immune to the sun* at the time, but I was always cold for like a couple decades before I got used to it, and I don't tan or burn, and I don't cast a shadow in the sun—my clothes do, and I cast a shadow under other kinds of light, but not in the sun. It also made my eyes black. I have since learned that lack of light should make your eyes *paler*, but like you said Ancient Greece wasn't known for being a logical place, except maybe Athens—pfft Athens."

"What color were they before?"

"Gold. People always used to compare them to the sun, so maybe that's why they turned black." I tried to picture Nikolas with gold eyes and tan skin and sun-bleached hair. I think he'd almost be glowing like that, like the sun incarnate. I would have liked to see it, but he was beautiful anyway, cool and pale and cheerful, adorable really. As I stared down at him, he smiled at me, but I noticed tears start to fall again.

"Nikolas, what's wrong now?" I asked, feeling worry bubbling in my chest. "I'm here for you."

"I've been alive so, so long, Ryden," Nikolas whimpered. "No one should be alive this long, it's too much pressure and I just ruin everything. It's my fault the gods are gone. I was supposed to remember them, but I kept forgetting, and then I . . . I forgot them on *purpose*. I thought that if they were gone, I'd die, but I didn't. People knew me, knew I was real, and so I kept on *being*."

"That's not on you Nikolas," I tried to comfort him. "If belief was all it took, then the gods screwed *themselves* by hiding away on their magic mountain and not interacting with anyone."

"But I was supposed to remember them, and I was supposed to win every war, I promised Ares I would always win, but I . . . sometimes I found myself fighting on the wrong side, and I just, I couldn't make myself help evil people win. I kept fighting in unjustified wars. I fought with Rome until it fell, and when I saw it falling, I didn't even *try* to stop it. I fought in Vietnam, both worlds wars, with the Mongols . . . It was . . . indescribable . . . wretched.

"War was brave and honorable back in Sparta, fighting for your people was the greatest thing you could do, but it's different now. It's so horrible, Ryden. People who died in battle were heroes, but they're just *ghosts* now, sometimes they don't even have names. Soldiers aren't people anymore—they're cannon fodder. All their values are superficial; there's no fighting for equality, and strength, and the good of the city-state; it's all about money now, in the end. And people kill and die over it.

"I promised I would always fight and win. When the recruiters said I didn't meet the height and weight requirements, I fought for the ability to fight, but Ryden, I can't do it anymore. I faked my death to leave Afghanistan, and I ran away. I *ran away* Ryden."

"It's okay, nobody blames you."

"There's nobody *left* to blame me."

Nikolas wept for a long time after that. I really do hate seeing him cry, but I could tell he needed it. He told me about the most horrible things that he'd been forced to live through, like after D-Day, when he'd discovered the stories about the Nazi concentration camps were true, and when he realized in Vietnam that he was on the wrong side of the fighting, and all the times when he'd fought and won, only to later discover that there was no good reason for the battles at all.

He told me about all the people he'd killed, and how it got easier over time, and then more and more difficult as he just got tired of it all, lost his will, and questioned his justifications. I think I'm the only one he's ever been able to talk to about any of this, and even though hearing about it made me feel sick, and there were some parts where I thought I might actually vomit, I managed to hold it together for Nikolas.

Late in the night, he finally cried himself to sleep, and I took him to bed. I'm not going to go into REM tonight. Normally, I would. I should, in order to stay healthy, but I can't just disappear. I need to still be here tomorrow, I think.

With resolve,

Ryden Brown

9

Raise a Glass to Firsts and Lasts

After hours and hours of reading, the sun had gone down, the lights were on in the living room, and Lucas was nearing the last few pages, flipping through loose leafs of college ruled binder paper, mostly, but there were a few pages of construction paper as well, and one entry was written on the back of a receipt.

After the entry from the day of the funeral, and the shorter one from the day after, Lucas had to take a moment to absorb it all. That had cinched it for him. There was no way that Grandpa Ryden could have guessed the exact date of his own funeral, and if that much was true, then the rest of it probably was too. His grandfather was—or had been—a time traveler; the Greek gods had once existed; there was a man named Nikolas Miracle, and he was immortal . . . and he would be at the funeral. Lucas might even be able to meet him.

Before that, though, he *had* to know how the story ended. As far as he knew, Grandpa Ryden had not time traveled during Lucas' lifetime, nor during his mother, Sophia's. No one could survive without REM sleep for more than eleven days, tops, and after three or four, sleep deprivation would kick in and could start to cause hallucinations, and though his sleep habits were odd, there was no denying that Grandpa had always been healthy, right up to the end. In that case, something must have happened. But what?

Lucas read about the time in 1447 when his grandfather couldn't understand old English, so he and Nikolas spoke Latin, and he fell off a horse—the day Nikolas believed they'd become a couple, and the day in 1964 Nikolas had mentioned, when Ryden freaked out over an unexpected kiss. It was also in 1964 that Ryden got vaccinated against smallpox, just in case. There was a mention of the day Ryden told Nikolas about his love of newspapers in 1796, and that the first one he'd read was *The New York Times*, which wasn't in print yet.

By the end, there were hundreds of entries ranging in length from a few words to several pages, and Ryden Brown had spent over a year bouncing unpredictably through time, never spending more than three days in any year.

Lucas' interest was piqued by an entry with an uncertain date. It wasn't the first entry in which his Grandfather hadn't been able to pin down the exact date on which he'd landed, but it was the earliest year so far, and one of the last entries, only a few pages from the end, written on both sides of a piece of blue construction paper in Grandpa Ryden's smallest hand. There was a tear from the bottom to almost halfway up the page, held together with brittle Scotch Tape, which rendered some of the words difficult to make out, and the edges which stuck out the sides of the cover were wrinkled, and faded to white.

December 476 or January 477 CE

I awoke in a bed which was basically an elevated mat, more like a cot than a bed really, in a wide, flat house somewhere in the ancient Roman Empire, though I didn't recognize it as such at first. I stepped out into the atrium around which the wide, one story home was built, and found my way to the exit. No one bothered me. The house, it seemed, was unoccupied.

If I were to guess, I'd say it had been that way for some time. Either the residents had moved, or else this was a summer home in the winter. The weather was nice, but I could definitely tell it was winter. The same kind of winter that I got back home where the sun was always shining upon the short days, and 60° F was bone-chillingly cold. I could smell the ocean—a familiar scent, mildly rancid but also pleasant for nostalgic reasons, and I knew I must be near a beach.

It wasn't long before I found myself walking on the beach, drawn there by instinct or absent-mindedness. I don't know which. There were few people there, and they were quiet. It was peaceful. As I walked, I wondered when I would run into Nikolas, as I always did.

I found him on a concrete sea wall, legs dangling over the side, fishing rod in hand, and watched him for a moment. Something seemed off, like he was upset, or maybe just obscenely exhausted—a feeling I've grown all too familiar with myself since the time-bouncing began.

I would have gone to him, but I didn't know how to get out to the sea wall, so I was forced to wait. It wasn't as though I was suffering however. The sand was coarser than I was used to, but even so, it would be difficult not to enjoy spending time on a Mediterranean beach. I stripped off some of the extra layers of my, frankly detestable, 2220s attire, and ambled into the waves in what amounted to a tunic and a pair of knee-length, skin-tight shorts. I'll never understand fashion.

Perhaps an hour or so later, and Nikolas hadn't moved an inch, when a voice came from behind me which was definitely not speaking English. I turned to see a man who would've been as tall as my shoulders, if he wasn't hunched with age, with leathery, middle-eastern skin, and clearly defined muscles which I'd like to think hadn't withered over time, because to think that they *had* would be somewhat frightening. In this time, in his prime, he would have been quite the imposing figure. It took me a moment to identify the language in which he spoke to me as Latin, and it was with great relief that I asked the man to repeat himself.

He asked who I was, and if I was a giant. I told him my name, and said that I was not. He asked where I was from, and I said far to the west, and then he asked me if I had a speech impediment, which I didn't understand at first, but eventually I answered that Latin wasn't my first language, though I'd thought I'd been getting better at it. Finally, he asked me if I knew Nikolas, though the way he pronounced the name was odd. Apparently he'd caught me looking at him. I said I did. He said he did too. I asked him how they'd met, grateful for anything to talk about, and he told me an interesting story then.

He said that his name was Darius, and he had been a slave, and that Rome had taken over his country many years ago, but that Nikolas had freed him, and now he was Nikolas' grateful friend and willing servant. He said that Nikolas had been a soldier until the Emperor Romulus Augustus was forced to flee, and Odoacer proclaimed himself the king of Italy (it was this knowledge which gave me a general idea of the date). Nikolas became one of the last to leave the Roman army.

When the dregs of the army were finally dissolved, Nikolas had simply left, moved away from the capitol to this town which shared land with the Mediterranean Sea, and Darius followed him. According to Darius' account, Nikolas said that this town would be a good place from which to watch as the once-great nation finished crumbling, as it had been doing for a hundred years.

He didn't seem that put-off by Nikolas' claim to have seen the last hundred years, and he told me that he'd been only twenty when Nikolas had freed him, almost forty years before. I had thought he was old for the era, but for a man to make it to nearly sixty in this time period was truly amazing.

I was listening to Darius' tale, so I didn't see Nikolas come off the sea wall and return to the shore, but then he was there, holding a fishing rod and a wooden bucket full of colorful fish I didn't recognize, which were probably extinct or evolved in my home-time. Nikolas' voice was much softer than I was used to when he greeted Darius. He still sounded kind, but there was something hollow about his tone, like he was empty inside.

"Salve, Nikolas!" I said, and moved in to hug him as I almost always did in greeting. I heard the hissing thud as the bucket of fish hit the sand and the next thing I knew, I was landing next to it, flat on my back, feeling bruises forming on my shoulder and chest, where Nikolas was holding me down, the end of the fishing rod buried deep in the sand next to my head.

I looked up in a daze of shock to meet a harsh glare like none I'd ever seen. In that moment, I felt in my soul that looks could kill. I could swear the raven black pools of his eyes were ready to swallow me up and drag me down to the underworld, while I drowned within them, too terrified to even move. I honestly thought I might die, right there, but Darius interrupted with a shout (I'm translating to English here, of course).

"He said he knew you!" Darius cried.

"I have never met this man," Nikolas said, not averting his dreadful glare. "How could he know me?"

"I can explain," I said, thoroughly terrified. "You may not believe me." Nikolas' eyes narrowed, and his suspicion was no less chilling than his glare. He made a sound, a half-hearted grunt, and got off me, picking up his bucket of fish, and letting me get up on my own.

"Dare not to touch me again, or—" and here he said something about fish and death and bones which sounded distinctly like a threat, and I felt distinctly threatened, but I didn't understand all of it. "Say what you will. You find there is little I cannot believe."

Here I feel I must express my embarrassment and apologies for my poor translating skills. It's one thing to have a conversation in Latin, but it's another entirely to translate that conversation to English.

I had realized by now, that this must be the earliest we would ever meet, and thought it was odd, since Nikolas had already been alive for several centuries by this point, that we hadn't met sooner. Nonetheless, I explained to Nikolas that I was from the future, and that every time I slept through the night, I woke up in a different time and place.

I told him that he was very dear to me in the future, that we'd meet again, and become close. I thought it best if I didn't reveal the nature of our relationship just yet, after all, to this Nikolas—Nikolaos, he corrected me. I suppose he must change it later on—I was a stranger. Nikolas went silent when I was done talking, and Darius, seeming to sense something I did not, offered to take the fish back to the home they apparently shared, and wash it. Nikolas nodded absently, never taking his eyes off of me.

Once we were alone, Nikolas said something, his expression totally blank, and his voice pensive. Basically it was, "you are the reason I keep living." I know he meant it *literally*, that he thought my existence, and the fact that we would meet again in the future, and my belief that he was real and alive was why he hadn't died yet, but to hear him say that made me smile.

He told me he no longer lived for Greece, nor for Rome, and that Darius was dying as all his friends and family and fellow soldiers had, as the gods had too, but that he would live as long as he was precious to me. I sensed an unsaid "whether I like it or not." I remembered what he'd told me a long time ago, about how I tended to show up in his darkest hour, when he needed me the most, and I wondered if this was what he meant.

This version of Nikolas seemed bitter and resentful, but more than anything, he seemed empty, and devoid of hope. I think that I was hope to him. I wasn't just the reason he couldn't die yet, but a reason for him to keep living. He invited me for a meal, in the end, and taught me the Roman rules of hospitality since I was, according to Darius, a clueless foreigner.

I'll sleep properly tonight, seeing as I don't mean much to this Nikolas, anyway. I'm a stranger that he knows he'll meet again, and I think the waiting is actually something he'll look forward to. So far, this is the earliest I've traveled, and it would seem that this is the earliest I will ever travel. I never realized how long Nikolas had lived before he met me. I feel sorry that I didn't come to him sooner. There's something else too; it feels ominous, though I don't know why.

With foreboding,

Ryden Brown

Lucas could feel that foreboding too. There were only three pages left of the journal.

10

What Happens When Time Runs Out

June 26, 1949

This is the third time I've landed in the 1940s, which is odd to say the least, but it's not the only odd thing to happen today. I haven't seen Nikolas at all today, and it's long after dark. I know he lived in New York City in 1949, and I even went to his home. I have a key, so I went inside, but he wasn't there. Not even Tetsudo was there, and he adopted the tortoise as a baby when he got home after the end of World War Two.

It doesn't make any sense. Nikolas has lived in the same place since 1775, he helped build this house with his own hands, and lived there as the city grew around it, first with the friend who helped him build it, and then alone after that friend passed away. He plumbed the whole house in 1870 and wired it in 1891, and had them both redone in the late seventies to replace the lead pipes and fix some faulty circuits. Even after he moved to LA in the fifties, he kept the deed to the place.

At least, I'm pretty sure he moved to LA in the mid-fifties . . . could he have moved earlier than I thought? But there was still food in the kitchen, *The New York Times* was delivered to the doorstep, and the place looks like it's been cleaned recently. Perhaps he's staying with friends today. He's a good person, and he always has at least one friend. I've met some of his friends, like Darius, and the crew of *The Blackbird*, and Nikolas is a good judge of character, so I'm sure he has friends that he visits with.

I've been waiting at his home for some time now. I read the paper, did the crossword to the best of my ability (Nikolas always knows more answers than I do, and I can't exactly Google things in 1949), and tuned in for most of a radio drama about a detective investigating an international insurance scam, which was either called *The Adventures of Frank Race*, or *The Shanghai Incident*, or maybe "The Shanghai Incident" was the name of the episode. That's probably it, actually, now that I think about it.

It's been dark out for a long time. Midnight is approaching. Nikolas still isn't back yet.

I'll sleep here tonight, and see him again when I wake up, I suppose, in another era. It's strange how much I've gotten used to seeing him every day. I feel like something's missing, not seeing him at all. I hope tomorrow comes soon, because this situation doesn't sit right with me.

With stress,

Ryden Brown

June 27, 1949

I woke up exactly where I fell asleep, one day later. I waited around, but Nikolas didn't come back today either.

June 28, 1949

I'm getting really worried now, not that I wasn't worried yesterday or the day before. Time has started progressing normally for me, and despite living in his house, I haven't seen Nikolas at all in three days. Perhaps he really has moved to LA already. If the same thing happens tomorrow, I'll go look for work, then save up enough to move out there. Maybe I'll enroll at San Diego State, where I was a student before all this started and finish my degree . . . . although I'd have to start over.

June 29, 1949

I went out and got a job today. It was almost laughably easy. I saw an ad in the paper asking for young men or women to work as wait-staff in some diner downtown, and just went over there, said I saw the ad in the paper, and that I'd been a waiter before, which I had done to supplement my scholarships in college, and Harold Jenkins, the owner, hired me on the spot. No resume or recommendations needed.

He did say, with an irritating tone of suspicion, that my skin was awful tan, to which I responded, "it is summer, sir," and that was that. I never felt that strongly either way about not really looking Latino or Filipino before all this, but I've been grateful for my German and English ancestry a lot for making me look white enough to pass, since I've found myself in past eras rife with discrimination.

I'm being paid 87 cents an hour for this job, plus tips, and Jenkins assured me that was pretty darn good, and that he always pays his workers well. I'll keep living in Nikolas' home for the time being, in case he comes back. It's not like I can get my own place yet, anyway, and I'm sure he wouldn't mind.

July 17, 1949

I haven't moved in time again, I just haven't had any reason to update my journal of late. I've almost saved up enough to move out to California, and I've sent a letter to what is now San Diego State *College*, but was San Diego State *University* in my home-time, describing my interest in enrolling next semester, and some of my qualifications, and asking about the requirements for admission. It was a pain to find the address at the library, but thankfully the librarian, Lavinia St. Clair, was a patient old woman, who helped me with the things I didn't understand.

I told Jenkins, the owner, that I'm planning on moving to the opposite coast next month, and he said that was a shame because I was very popular among the ladies who frequented the diner. I had to bite my tongue against a sarcastic comment or a gay joke, as I've had to do so many times since I started working in his establishment.

Jenkins is a nice man, and a great cook, but he's taken to trying to set me up with every lady who even bats her eyelashes in my general direction, which is pretty frustrating to say the least. Despite my frequent claims that I am spoken for, he says that he'll only believe me when he meets my lady.

Having to be so thoroughly closeted after being out and proud since middle school is a constant struggle, and I think if I have to keep holding back my remarks, I might bite my tongue off completely. I told him my "lady" lived in California, which was why I was moving out there as soon as I had the money. He seemed to accept that, though I don't think his efforts to pair me up with the patrons will stop.

Even though I've almost saved up enough to move, I'm going to wait a couple weeks to see if I hear back from the college before I pack my meager belongings and catch a plane to the opposite coast.

With hope,

Ryden Brown

July 23, 1949

I heard back from the college. They said that I sounded like an unusual case, but that they were interested in interviewing me, and seeing how I score on some of their aptitude tests. I expect I'll do fine, given that my education is undoubtedly more advanced than their average applicant. I'll probably get marks taken off for knowing things that haven't been discovered or confirmed yet, if anything.

I bought my ticket today, and I'll be taking off for LA on the thirtieth.

July 30, 1949

I'm on the plane to LA, and I'll be arriving late tonight. I left a note in Nikolas' home, just in case I'm wrong, and he hasn't moved yet. If all goes well, I'll be enrolled in college, and won't be able to move back.

July 31, 1949

The house Nikolas should be living in is owned by an elderly couple named Diane and Michael Wethers. So he hasn't moved to LA yet after all.

It was unwise of me to try to chase after him. Rereading some old entries, I remembered that Nikolas said he could sense me when I appeared, and usually, he was the one to find me when I showed up, not the other way around. I never had to look for him before, so . . . . I'll just have to wait.

I'm going to find a place in San Diego, close to the school, and hope that he finds me, like he always does.

August 2, 1949

I had my tests and interview with the college today. I'm pretty sure I was right about getting a few answers wrong because I knew better than the administrators, but it wasn't enough to drastically affect my score. They said they couldn't say for sure, but it seemed likely that I'd be admitted, and that I'd hear from them one way or the other via letter. I gave them the address of the apartment I found yesterday.

December 25, 1949

I know it's been a few months. I got into college. I'm studying history with the goal of eventually earning a teaching degree, just as I had been doing in my home-time. It's Christmas Day, and I am alone. My roommate, Daniel, went home to his family for the holidays, but no one in my family has been born yet, at least no one I know, so I have no one to go home to. I haven't seen Nikolas at all since the time-bouncing stopped. I got him a Christmas present, but it's sitting on the table, unopened.

I miss him so much it hurts. It feels like I'm missing a lung, or something else *vitally* important. Sometimes I wonder if any of it was even real, but it *had* to have been real. I read my old entries over and over and remind myself that it was definitely real. That it definitely happened.

The greatest gap year ever has ended pretty miserably, but every time I think of it, of him, I do everything I can to convince myself that I'll see him again. The man's immortal, so if I just live long enough, we'll meet again sometime, even by accident.

January 1, 1950

New Year's Eve passed by without a kiss. I cried through a lot of it, drank the entire bottle of champagne Daniel left me. Needless to say, I have a headache. This will be my last entry until I meet Nikolas again, but I *will* meet him again. I'm sure I will. I have to.

With certainty,

Ryden Brown

That was the final entry.

Lucas stared at it for a long time.

Did that mean that Grandpa Ryden *hadn't* met Nikolas again?

That couldn't be how it ended. That was too sad. He got just over one year with Nikolas, constantly jumping through time, having all their encounters in a different order from each other, and they didn't get to stay together in the end? They didn't get a happily ever after?

But then, would it have been a 'happily ever after' if they had? Nikolas would have had to watch Ryden grow old and die, just like everyone else in his life had. Grandpa Ryden would have grown into an old, old man, while Nikolas was still as young as the day they met. Grandma Eileen would have married someone else, and there was no way of knowing if that person would have been good for her or not. Lucas, his mother, and his older brother wouldn't have been born.

Even taking all that into account, Lucas couldn't make himself be satisfied with that. That wasn't how the story ended, it couldn't be. If Grandpa Ryden was gay, and he'd said as much in the journal, then why had he married Grandma Eileen anyway? Why hadn't Nikolas been at his home in New York? How come he'd never come looking for Ryden? Ryden had lived to be over a hundred, and Nikolas was immortal, so it wasn't like he hadn't had the time.

The more he thought about it, the more frustrated he became. He had to know the answers. He *had* to know, but how could he find out, and as soon as possible?

Nikolas would be at Grandpa Ryden's funeral, Lucas remembered, but that was the day after tomorrow. In the meantime, he could think of only one other person who might know something. It was nearly two am now, so he reluctantly dragged himself off to bed, but come a reasonable hour, he would go to his mother, and ask her what she knew.

11

Go Ask Your Mother

Lucas knocked on his mother's door.

"Coming!" he heard her voice call. Sophia Brown lived near downtown on the other side of the city from her father and youngest son. It was late morning, and Lucas had driven there shortly after waking up. He had left the journal at home, figuring if she didn't already know about it, there was no way she would believe him. His mother was a highly skeptical woman.

"Oh, hi Lucas." Her eyebrows lifted in surprise when she saw him, before she pulled the door all the way open and stepped aside to let him in. "Come on in."

"Thanks, Mom."

"It's not like you to drop by unexpectedly, what's this all about?" See? Skeptical.

"I wanted to ask you about Grandpa Ryden," Lucas told her. There was no point beating around the bush with his mother. She never let anything happen without knowing why first, and she'd always had a way of wheedling information out of her boys as long as either Lucas or his older brother could remember, so it was better to just say things outright.

His mother's expression softened into affectionate pity. "Of course dear. Have you had breakfast? Would you like anything."

"No thanks, I'm alright." She frowned.

"Well I'm going to get some hot cocoa, and I'm making you some too, because I know you'll drink it, even if you say you don't want any. You don't fool me." Lucas' lips quirked into a smile and he followed his mother into the kitchen, taking a seat at the kitchen table while she set a kettle boiling and poured cocoa mix into a pair of mugs. "Now, what did you want to ask?"

"What happened to him after he went to college? And how'd he meet Grandma Eileen? What was he like when you were a kid?"

"Okay, slow down there," his mom held up a hand to stop him. "I'll tell you what I can, but I don't know my dad's whole life story." Lucas nodded.

"I can tell you that after college, he took a job as a history teacher at a local high-school, and he worked there until, well until the other day. Mom and I tried to get him to retire every summer for the last twenty years of her life. He was old, and he had plenty of money, since he always seemed to make really smart investments. He could have stopped teaching a long time ago, but he didn't, because he loved it.

"As for how he met your grandma, well, that's a bit of a scandalous story, see she was his student. They weren't involved then, but they were friends, and they stayed in touch after she graduated. One thing led to another, and they got married in 1969. He was almost twenty years older than her at the time."

"Hold on, that's it?" Lucas asked. "The whole story is 'one thing led to another' and that's *it*?"

"Yeah, sorry I don't have any more details. That's always how Mom and Dad told it. She was his student, and they kept in touch after she graduated, and 'one thing led to another.'" She shrugged and turned to the kettle as it started to whistle. She poured the boiling water into the mugs and then opened a drawer to get some spoons. "I'm disappointed too, trust me. After I met your father, I hounded them for details on why they decided to get married, I thought it might help me decide if he was 'the one,' but all they'd ever say was 'one thing led to another.'"

She placed both cups of cocoa on the table and took a seat next to Lucas. "I don't know exactly what things led to what other things, but from what I've been able to piece together, they might've been dating in secret, and then mom got pregnant, and that's why they decided to get married, because I was born only seven months later. Grandma said she had no idea they were involved like that until they announced their engagement, and she opposed it at first, because she didn't want her daughter marrying a man twice her age, but Mom insisted."

That theory did not match up with Lucas' expectations at all. He felt his eyebrows scrunch up in thought and he took a sip of his cocoa. "Do you know anything about your paternal grandparents?" he asked.

"No, Dad said they died. Actually what he said was they weren't alive, now that I think about it. He never actually said how, either." *That* sounded more like Grandpa Ryden. "What was the other thing you asked? What was he like when I was a kid?"

"Yeah."

"Well, let's see. Mom always told me about how, when I was a baby, Dad would always help out taking care of me, and doing housework and cooking, and when she said that was *her* job, he said he refused to be a useless husband. She told me about how she'd meet up with her friends and feel guilty that she'd married a man so good about those things, because their husbands were all layabouts who wouldn't change a diaper to save their lives." She blew on her cocoa, thinking about what else she could tell him.

"He was like that a lot. I remember he'd complain that it was always just mothers who came to parent nights, and joined the PTA and everything, because all these uninvolved fathers reflected badly on fathers as a whole."

"That tracks." Lucas chuckled, remembering hearing similar rants since he moved in to be Grandpa Ryden's caretaker. Last year there had been one dad on the PTA, and Grandpa Ryden was so proud of him, and subsequently even more disappointed in the other dads. Though he had been noticing a steady incline in the number of dads showing up to school events, and seemed to approve.

"He still does that huh?" His mother smiled into her cocoa, but when she pulled the mug away, the smile was gone. "Or . . . I guess not anymore." There was a sullen silence for a moment as they both sipped their cocoa again and tried not to think about the difference between 'does' and 'did.' Lucas cleared his throat, his mother rubbed her eyes.

"What else can you tell me?"

"Oh, well, he was really smart, and not just about history, although I'm sure you know he was more passionate about history than anything else," she said. "He taught me how to read before I can even remember, and he would almost always answer my questions, even if Mom said that I wasn't old enough to know the answers. Although, there were a few mistakes that he made a lot, like he always forgot to include Pluto when he was listing planets.

"You know what else? Dad was always so accepting, and really open and progressive about pretty much everything. He was always so encouraging, especially to his students, and I think he sort of rubbed that off on the people around him, just by virtue of being so nice about it. You know he was the faculty advisor for the GSA at his school as soon as they started it a couple years back."

"Yeah, I remember the day he came home complaining about how the principal thought that a younger teacher would be more suited to the position, even though the students asked for him specifically, so he planned a weeks worth of lessons on exclusively queer history, and had to wade through angry emails from a handful of really pissed off parents."

"Oh my," his mother barked a laugh. "Did he really? I hadn't heard that one."

"Yeah . . . hey, were he and Grandma Eileen . . . were they *happily* married?" He felt kinda bad asking something like that, but he still wanted to know.

"What? Of course they . . . well, they seemed happy enough, anyway . . ." She looked away from him, sipped her cocoa, frowned at the kitchen table, and generally looked like she had never thought about it before. "I don't think they were *unhappy*, but . . . well . . . I never saw my parents kiss each other.

"I can't think of even a single time they kissed, at least not in front of me. And as a kid, I didn't think much of it, but once I got to grow up a little, I started to realize how odd it was. They never were all that physically affectionate with each other that I can remember. Oh, never mind. I'm reading too much into it. It's probably that they just didn't feel comfortable with PDA. Why would you ask me something like that?"

"Do you know anything about someone named Nikolas Miracle?" Lucas asked.

"That character Dad used to teach you and your brother history when you were little?" Lucas looked at his mother, stunned, for a moment.

"What?"

"That's the little guy who started in Ancient Greece, and then won immortality from the gods, so he lived through all of history, right?" His mother looked back at him, confused. "Dad used to use him as a teaching device. Like those shows that teach math and science to kids? Nikolas was just *Bill Nye the Science Guy*, but for history—and he wasn't a real person."

"*What?*" Lucas demanded again.

"Yeah. Nikolas Miracle goes to America on a boat, and there are angry rats, and people are dying of smallpox, but the new world holds the promise of a better tomorrow. Nikolas Miracle storms the beaches of Normandy on D-Day with his spunky crew of soldiers who eat carrots and read comic books. Nikolas Miracle is a pirate on a ship called *The Blackbird*, and when they're not pillaging and plundering, they put on plays to entertain themselves. He told me those stories too, back in grade-school. I loved 'em. They helped me remember the details. Honestly, they're probably the main reason I passed history in school."

So *that* was why the name sounded familiar. Grandpa Ryden had told people about Nikolas; he'd just presented him as a fictional character. He probably used those stories to remember Nikolas, and to share him with his loved ones, even though he couldn't tell anyone the truth. He presented them as fiction, as a teaching device, which was just like Grandpa Ryden.

"Why are you asking about that?" His mother asked.

"I read the name recently, in Grandpa's things, and couldn't figure out why it sounded familiar," Lucas answered vaguely. "What else can you tell me about Grandpa Ryden?" The two swapped stories for a while longer, had lunch, and eventually, Lucas went home.

When he got there, he plopped down on his favorite armchair with a sigh. His mother had answered *some* questions, but not all of them. She couldn't tell Lucas why her father stopped time traveling. She didn't know he had time traveled to begin with. She couldn't say why Grandpa Ryden never met Nikolas again, because she didn't know Nikolas was a real person.

Lucas looked at the journal, still sitting on the coffee table. Just to the right of the journal was the box of letters he'd also taken out of the attic. He hadn't looked at them yet, except to confirm what they were. He figured he might as well. Opening the box, he picked up the letter on the top.

Dearest Eileen,

It's only been two days since I last saw your beautiful, smiling face, but it feels like forever. I miss you like I missed the target in the first week of basic training—all the time. I can't wait to see you and our baby when I get back home, and when I do, I'll marry you on the spot. I love you with everything, more than you can believe.

Alex C.

Who in the world was Alex C? Lucas looked in puzzlement at the letter. He turned over the envelope to look at the sender. The letter appeared to be from someone named Alexander Castellanos, and it was sent from Vietnam. There were thirteen letters from him in total, and after that, a yellow card—a telegram saying that Alexander Castellanos had been killed in action. Behind that, a pair of letters with the envelopes stamped "return to sender" addressed to Alexander Castellanos from Eileen Shanon.

12

Differing Opinions of the Phrase 'The End'

When the day of the funeral finally arrived, Lucas spent the morning anxiously cleaning Grandpa Ryden's house from top to bottom. Since he was young, he'd always cooked or cleaned when he was nervous, or had something on his mind. His mother used to sign him up for things like youth programs and school events so that she'd get a clean house the day before. It wasn't until high school that he'd caught on to her scheme, but when he did he remembered being so angry that he refused to speak to her for a week.

Knowing the story so far, it wouldn't be hard to guess what was on his mind as he scrubbed the grease from the stove top and dusted his grandfather's numerous bookshelves. He'd discovered two days before that his grandfather was a time traveler from the 2180s, who had somehow gotten stuck in 1949. He'd discovered yesterday that his grandfather was not, biologically speaking, his grandfather at all. And he had no idea what he might discover that very day.

In just a few short hours, Lucas had a chance to meet the one person who might actually be able to answer his questions. The one person who might be able to explain everything to him. The one person who might know how the story ends.

One o' clock came around with agonizing slowness, but when it finally did, Lucas put the journal and the box of letters into a bag and got in his car to drive to the church where Grandma Eileen had been buried. The minister said nice things over a clean, grey casket. Lucas' mother said some words of her own. Lucas' older brother Gregory, who had flown in all the way from Massachusetts to attend, left some white flowers on top of the casket.

There were a lot more people than Lucas had expected there to be, friends, coworkers, former students, current students, people Lucas didn't even recognize. Grandpa Ryden was a well loved man. Many of them walked up to the front of the church to speak, their wavering voices echoed under the vaulted ceilings. They talked about how he was always so kind, and so accepting, and how he knew how to have a good time. All had only pleasant things to say.

A girl from a group of teenagers who didn't seem to be accompanied by any adults walked up to the front, encouraged by her friends, and said that even though he was just her history teacher, Mr. Brown was like a father to her, and better to her than her real family ever was, and that she would never forget him as long as she lived. Tears streamed down her face as she left the stage and walked into the comforting arms of her waiting friends.

In the very back of the room, behind the dozens of people who had come to the proceedings, Lucas saw a small man, dressed in a long, black coat, pale as a ghost, with pitch black eyes and a solemn expression.

Could that be him? Lucas thought. He looked down at the bag in his lap, at the box of letters written to his grandmother from a man who was not his grandfather, but also was, even though no one knew but him. He looked at the journal which he hadn't really planned to read, but that he'd brought anyway.

He remembered another letter, one tucked between the pages on an entry from June fifth, 1944, written to the man now lying in a casket, from someone who truly loved him, with instructions to read it when he knew he wouldn't see him again, a letter in a yellowing envelope which was torn but never fully opened.

He opened the journal and took out the letter, tearing carefully at the brittle envelope, and unfolding the pages within. He read it to himself, while others stood before the crowd and told their own stories about his grandfather. And when everyone was done, and it was finally Lucas' turn as it had been decided beforehand that he would be the last to speak, he walked forward, journal in hand, and read the letter again.

"Thank you all for saying everything that needed to be said, everything that could be said, of my Grandpa Ryden. I'm going to finish this off now, by reading a letter written to him by someone he loved dearly." Lucas looked to the man in the back of the chapel, whose pitch black eyes he could see clearly, even from all the way across the room.

"'Ryden, my dearest love,'" the letter began, and Lucas saw the haunting eyes of the man in the back widen with recognition. "'I know that I will not die tomorrow, as I have not died in any of the countless other battles that I have fought, but my greatest fear is that eventually a time will come, after which we will not meet again, and should that happen, there are things I want to tell you.'" Lucas saw his mother in the front row, her eyebrows scrunched up in confusion. She didn't have to be Sherlock Holmes to know that her own mother had not been the one to write this letter.

"'You may not know this yet, my dear, but meeting you saved my life. I thank you every single day for being my salvation, and for giving me a reason to look forward to every tomorrow. Your kindness has made me a better person, and your gentle touch has always led me in the right direction. Every day I spend with you is the best day of my life. I only wish those days weren't so few, and far between.

"'I want to tell you what you mean to me, but the words don't exist to describe the importance of your role in my life. I don't want to tell you how dark the path I might have followed is, had I not met you, but you should know.

"'I had a family once, long ago, whom I barely remember, and I've lost a thousand friends, but of all the many people that I've known, I've known you the longest—and the briefest. And if, when you grow old, as everyone seems to do, your memory fades, and you forget all you once knew about me, please remember this one thing: I love you, Ryden. I have loved you for five hundred years, and gods be willing, I will love you for a thousand yet, or more.

"'Live well, my dear, when I am no longer with you. Do not let my absence hinder your laughter or sour your smile. I have plenty of practice loving you from a distance, so just remember that, and let yourself be happy wherever you are.'" Lucas swallowed as the letter came to a close. "'With love, Nikolas Miracle.'" He finished, and folded the letter back into its envelope, tucking it between the pages in his grandfather's journal.

When Lucas, his older brother, and two of their grandfather's good friends carried the casket out to the churchyard, there wasn't a dry eye to be seen. When the casket was lowered into the ground, there was no shame to be found in weeping openly for such a man as Ryden Brown.

"Where did you find that letter?" Gregory demanded. Lucas looked at his brother, blurry through his tears.

"In the attic, in a journal from when Grandpa Ryden was younger," he said.

"I didn't know . . ." Gregory trailed off, but Lucas understood, and pulled him into a hug.

"Nobody did," he whispered.

"Lucas!" he heard his mother shout, and she jogged up to him. She stopped, wiping at her eyes. "Lucas, is that what all those questions were about yesterday?" he pulled out of the hug and nodded.

"I found those other letters you mentioned. You said he read some at Grandma Eileen's funeral." He reached into his bag, pulled out the box, and handed it to her. "I think you should read them yourself. Now, excuse me for a minute."

He ran out to the edges of the crowd, looking for the stranger who'd been standing in the back of the room. He didn't see him at first, but when he finally caught sight of the small figure, all he could see was the back of his long, black coat, walking away, almost unnoticed. People kept trying to stop Lucas and offer their condolences. It took him a few moments to break away to catch the stranger. Finally, he called out to him.

"Nikolas!" The stranger stopped, and Lucas was finally able to catch up, stopping just a few feet away. "You are Nikolas, aren't you? Nikolas Miracle?" There was a beat of silence where Lucas thought the man would turn to face him, but he didn't.

"I am." Lucas took another step closer.

"So all of it really was true, about the time traveling, about you and him?" Lucas saw Nikolas' head nod. "And you're really immortal?" Another nod. Another step forward. "Do you know what happened? Back in 1949? Do you know what made him stop moving?"

"The time ran out," Nikolas said quietly.

"What does that mean?"

"The time ran out," he repeated louder. Finally, Nikolas turned to face Lucas. He seemed even smaller up close, but his voice was deeper than Lucas had expected, and his eyes were much more intense. The way they had been described in the journal, Lucas had thought they would be softer, but maybe they were only soft when he was looking at Grandpa Ryden. "It stopped jumping about, it stopped glitching, or bouncing, or whatever it was doing to Ryden that made him fall asleep in one era and wake up in another.

"It slowed to a crawl. He stopped moving through it, and started following its flow. Whatever tether held the two of us together snapped, and I had to let him live his life."

"Why didn't you find him? In his journal it said that he left you a note at your house in New York."

"The same morning that he landed in New York, I left for France to comfort a friend on his deathbed," Nikolas explained. "When I returned to find his note, I knew that something changed. Once he stopped time-traveling, he wasn't *my* Ryden anymore, not really. I knew I'd see him again during his own lifetime, and that would be *my* Ryden."

"I don't get to be a *part* of time, I only really get to watch, and it's a terrible thing to see but not experience. Being with Ryden, that was an experience, more real and more vivid than anything I'd felt in centuries, but after the time ran out, I had to let him go. Let him have his own experiences, and trust that I'd see him out of time again."

"So you never looked for him, never tried to find him, or spend time with him?" Lucas asked, almost offended on his grandfather's behalf.

"I moved all the way out to California just because he was here," Nikolas scoffed. "I stopped in LA 'cause I knew if I was any closer, I wouldn't be able to stay away. Close enough, but not too close. Close enough that I met his wife once. She had a toddler with her. That was your mother. Close enough that I could attend his funeral."

"My mom's not really his," Lucas said, thinking it might be of some consolation. "Her real dad died in Vietnam. I . . . I don't know all the details, but it seems like Grandpa Ryden married Grandma Eileen so that she wouldn't have to raise a kid on her own on top of having just lost the man she loved and wanted to marry."

"Is that so?" Nikolas said, and he seemed a little relieved. He had an expressive voice which couldn't hide his emotions well at all.

"Do you miss him?" It was a stupid question, Lucas realized, but there it was.

"More than I can say," Nikolas answered anyway. "I always miss him when he's gone, but I'll see him again, and so will you, if you keep an eye out." Lucas nodded, and just as Nikolas started to leave again, he thought of one more thing he had to say.

"Wait! You should know . . . that letter wasn't opened," he said. Nikolas looked at him, eyes wide with surprise. "You told him to open it when he thought he'd never see you again, but he never opened it. Right up until the end, he never gave up on seeing you again. He really loved you." Nikolas' mouth dropped open ever so slightly, and he blinked a few times.

"I . . ." he started to say, but he was at a loss for words.

"I think you should have this," Lucas said, and took out the journal, holding it out for Nikolas to take. "And um, if you could say hello to him for me, next time you see him . . . tell him thanks, or maybe just give him a hug?"

"I can do that," Nikolas said, accepting the journal. He flipped through it, glancing page by page, then when he reached the end, he handed it back. "Thank you for this, but I'd rather be surprised. I know when the last time I meet him will be, so I can decide whether or not to remember it. Maybe I'll write it down and put it in a box, and open that box up again in a thousand years, or perhaps I'll decide to set the box on fire.

"Keep it, Lucas. Tell it as a bedtime story, pass it down as a family heirloom, or bury it in a time capsule for future historians to find and wonder about." Nikolas smiled, though it didn't reach his unsettling, coal-colored eyes. "I don't want to know how it ends just yet, because for me, it isn't over. Goodbye, Lucas."

"Goodbye, Nikolas Miracle." Lucas stood there and watched, journal in hand, as Nikolas walked away, and once he turned the corner, he heard his brother's voice behind him.

"Was that really him?" Gregory asked. "I kinda caught the last of what you said, sorry."

"Yeah, that was him."

"Do you remember those stories Grandpa used to tell us, about Nikolas Miracle as a gladiator in the Roman coliseum, and fighting for The Union during the Civil War, and that stuff?" Gregory asked. Lucas didn't remember those stories very well, but then, Gregory would have been older when Grandpa Ryden told them, so he would remember them better.

"You should read this," Lucas said simply, and handed the journal to Gregory. "It's Grandpa Ryden's journal—the one I found that letter in. It's kind of unbelievable, but it's all true."

"What's unbelievable?" Gregory asked, accepting it.

"You'll see when you read it," Lucas said. "And be careful not to damage it because it's super old."

"Yeah, sure thing, and I'll be sure to get it back to you when I'm done." Lucas just nodded, still staring absently at where Nikolas had disappeared, until Gregory threw his arm over his brother's shoulders, and brought him back into the throng of their grandfather's numerous loved ones.

www.ingramcontent.com/pod-product-compliance
Lightning Source LLC
Chambersburg PA
CBHW022023120726
47898CB00008BA/2853